Callum had b
appraisal.

He waited until [...] with some amusement, 'And do you [...] surgery, young Dr Greenwood?'

Nancy raised her eyebrows at his terminology and as their eyes met—his rueful, hers questioning— she suddenly burst out laughing. 'Young Dr Greenwood is fine, thank you very much,' she told him gravely. 'She adores your fish tank, and she's just itching to get into that playpen!'

'Did I sound very patronising?' he asked her seriously.

'No. You sounded—um—'

'Paternal?'

No, certainly *not* paternal!

Sharon Kendrick had a variety of jobs before training as a nurse and a medical secretary, and found that she enjoyed working in a caring environment. She was encouraged to write by her doctor husband after the birth of their two children and much of her medical information comes from him and from friends. She lives in Surrey where her husband is a GP. She has previously written medical romances as Sharon Wirdnam and now, as Sharon Kendrick, divides her time between the medical romances and Mills & Boon Presents.

Recent titles by the same author:

WAIT AND SEE
TAKING IT ALL
TAKING RISKS
CONSULTANT CARE

ALL THE CARE
IN THE WORLD

BY
SHARON KENDRICK

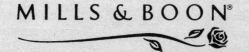

MILLS & BOON®

To the three greatest influences on my
nursing career. . .Mandy Gregory,
Ella Scott and Kingsley Lawrence.

*First published in Great Britain 1998
Harlequin Mills & Boon Limited,
Eton House, 18-24 Paradise Road, Richmond, Surrey TW9 1SR*

© Sharon Kendrick 1998

ISBN 0 263 80704 5

*Set in Times 10 on 12 pt. by
Rowland Phototypesetting Limited
Bury St Edmunds, Suffolk*

03-9803-45939-D

*Printed and bound in Great Britain
by Mackays of Chatham PLC, Chatham*

CHAPTER ONE

THE paperwork which greeted the return of Callum Hughes from his skiing holiday was piled so high on his desk that he was seriously afraid it might collapse into a muddled heap all over his surgery floor.

He shouldn't have cut it so fine, he thought. And if his flight from France hadn't been delayed until the early hours of this morning then he might have been able to tackle all this before surgery began.

He dropped his briefcase on the floor and said something rather impolite underneath his breath as he quickly divided the pile into two.

'Sorry?' said Jenny McDavid, his practice manager, whose comfortable, plump appearance belied her briskly efficient manner. She had followed him into the room with a long list of telephone message for Purbrook Surgery's most popular doctor. 'What was that you said, Dr Hughes?'

'Unrepeatable,' growled Callum, his craggy face lighting up as one of the receptionists came into the surgery, bearing an enormous cup of steaming coffee. 'Oh, thanks, Judy,' he murmured gratefully. 'Just what I need! I don't suppose there's any chance of a biscuit?'

'I bought you a Danish from the bakery on my way into work,' dimpled Judy, her expression as eager as a teenager's instead of a grandmother of two. 'In case you missed breakfast. As you so often *do*, Doctor!' she remonstrated gently. 'I'll go and get it!' And she sped

5

out of the office to return minutes later with a succulent concoction, glistening with lemon syrup and studded with nuts and raisins.

'Mmm,' said Callum ecstatically, as he bit into it. 'Thanks, Judy!' he called after the receptionist's retreating form.

Jenny shook her head with a look of mock bewilderment. 'I just don't know how you do it, Callum Hughes,' she told him sternly. 'I really don't.'

'Do what?' he queried, an innocent smile lightening his face as he lowered his large frame into the chair with surprising grace for so tall a man.

'Have every woman in this practice eating out of your hand—'

'Surely it's me eating out of *her* hand!' he joked, holding the pastry aloft.

'Running around after you,' continued Jenny, trying her best to sound severe but failing spectacularly when confronted by the distracting dazzle of his green eyes. 'Buying your meals and doing your shopping,' she continued. 'And collecting your shirts from the dry-cleaners—'

'But I'm a busy man!' he protested.

'And they are busy women!' she retorted. 'With homes and families of their own to run.'

'On what grounds are you objecting, Jenny?' he asked mildly, as he fixed her with a stare from his narrowed green eyes. 'Am I exploiting them? Well, am I?'

Jenny pursed her lips as she silently acknowledged the ridiculously over-generous bonuses he gave to each staff member every Christmas. She had to admit that most of them would have run round after him if he had just given them one of his heart-warming smiles! 'No, you're not exploiting them,' she agreed reluctantly, 'but. . .'

Callum's green eyes twinkled mischievously. 'But?'

'It's about time you found yourself a wife, Callum Hughes!' Jenny declared boldly.

Callum clutched dramatically at his throat with an expression of horror. 'Don't allow anyone with feminist principles hear you say *that*, Mrs McDavid!' he declared. 'The implication being that the principal duty of a wife is to run around after her husband—'

'And isn't it?' asked Jenny cynically.

He shook his dark head and overlong strands of hair tickled his suntanned neck, reminding him that he really should have found the time to have a haircut before coming back to work. 'Not at all.' He shook his dark head. 'Marriage should be an equal partnership.'

'You really believe that?'

'I really do,' he agreed solemnly, though that irrepressible glint was still lurking in the depths of his green eyes.

'Then no wonder you've remained single all this time,' sighed Jenny as she stared into his craggily handsome face, thinking that if ever Dr Hughes *did* get around to marrying the woman who finally won him over would be fortunate indeed. She glanced down at the list in her hand. 'Here are your messages.'

'Anything urgent?'

She shook her head as she scanned the list. 'Not really. We dealt with all the most pressing stuff. And—oh.' Her face became slightly wary, as if she was the bearer of bad news. 'Mr Petersham, the general surgeon from St Saviour's, rang to say that he had operated on Emma Miles. He spoke to Dr Davenport—'

She halted in mid-flow as Callum lifted one hand for silence and with the other punched out the extension number of his partner. But she wasn't offended by his occasionally peremptory approach—Callum Hughes was such a brilliant doctor that he could get away with *murder*, she thought.

'David?' said Callum. 'Sorry to disturb you, but I've just got back and I believe you spoke to Mike Petersham at St Saviour's?'

'Yes, that's right,' came the voice of his partner.

'And?' But the strained quality of those three words told Callum that the prognosis was bleak, as he had feared.

'He wanted you to know that your suspected diagnosis of carcinoma of the stomach was correct,' said David reluctantly. 'He has operated and done just about everything he can, but it doesn't look very good. I'm terribly sorry, Callum. I know how close you are to Emma and her family.'

Callum went through the motions of thanking his colleague, then put the phone down and shook his dark head as if in denial. Two deep frown marks furrowed deep lines on his forehead. 'Damn!' he protested on a groan, reflecting—not for the first time—how fundamentally unfair life could be. 'Damn and damn and damn!'

'Bad?' said Jenny.

The practice manager was too intelligent not to know everything that was going on in the various surgeries. She was also the soul of discretion. 'Worse than bad,' grated Callum, feeling raw with the pain of such unwelcome knowledge. 'Emma is far too young and beautiful to have contracted something like this. Is she still in hospital?'

Jenny nodded. 'She is—on Poplar Ward. Will you go and see her?'

'Of course I will,' he sighed, as he thought of Emma's youth and determination and beauty. He felt like raging against an uncaring God, but that would do her no good. Nor him. Nor the rest of his patients, some of whom would infuriate him with their insignificant little problems which were nothing compared to what Emma was going to have to endure during the next however many months she had left to live.

He made a mental note to ask Judy or one of the other receptionists to buy him a bunch of flowers to take with him. Or maybe she would prefer a book?

'That's probably the most pressing thing,' Jenny continued gently. 'The library at the hospital rang to say that they've managed to trace that new paper on asthma you wanted. Oh, and your new registrar rang up to say that she's looking forward to her first morning with you. That's this morning,' she added helpfully.

Callum narrowed his eyes, briefly disconcerted by hearing the hospital term which sounded so out of place in his surgery. 'My new *what*?' he demanded.

'Your registrar,' explained Jenny patiently. 'Your new GP registrar—'

'You mean my trainee?'

'Oh, don't be such a stick-in-the-mud, Callum! That's their brand-new title! You must move with the times, you know!' reprimanded Jenny tartly, until she realised that he was teasing her yet again. 'Why did they chance the title from GP Trainee to GP Registrar?' she asked him curiously. 'Do you know?'

'Patients thought that the word "trainee' meant that they were still students,' he answered, 'instead of fully qualified doctors who were about to add another three years of experience while they trained to become general practitioners.'

Jenny nodded, something in the tone of his voice making her question him further. 'And was that the only reason?'

Callum shrugged his massively broad shoulders as he began to pull the first pile of paperwork towards him. 'I think a lot of junior doctors were also a little unhappy with the word "trainee",' he mused.

'They said that it made them sound like a would-be chef or butcher, instead of a highly qualified individual with over seven years' doctoring underneath their belts! This puts them on a par with their hospital colleagues and stops them feeling like the poor relations of medicine.'

'And is that the case?' asked Jenny in surprise.

Callum nodded. 'Oh, undoubtedly. General practice has suffered from intellectual rubbishing by hospital staff for much too long now. And it's time that we stood up and showed the world that we're proud to be general practitioners.'

'Yes, Dr Hughes,' said Jenny, hiding a smile which bordered on the wistful. It was such a waste, she thought fleetingly, that a man as good-looking and as gorgeous as Dr Callum Hughes should channel all his passion and his energy into his job!

'Anyway, she'll be here at about eleven,' she continued equably. 'I told her to arrive later than we would usually expect—explained that you were just back from holidays and that you'd have a lot of catching up to do.

I said it was probably best to come *after* surgery on her first morning, rather than throwing her straight in at the deep end. I do hope that's all right?'

Callum was frowning at a rather bolshie letter from a consultant who had recently moved into the area. Though his surgical reputation was good, he clearly wasn't the world's greatest diplomat! 'Hmm? Yes, that's fine, Jenny,' he said absently, and then, as he heard the practice manager head towards the door, he lifted his head and said, 'What's her name, by the way?'

'It's Nancy,' said Jenny. 'Nancy Greenwood.'

'Pretty name,' he commented, with a smile.

'Yes,' agreed Jenny, wondering why fate didn't lend a hand by sending Dr Hughes a *single* doctor instead of one who was married! 'You met her when she asked to be transferred from the Southbury scheme. Remember?'

Callum looked up, screwing his green eyes up in such a way that even his cynical practice manager's heart began to pound rather erratically.

He was relatively new at training prospective general practitioners, and he had interviewed so few that it didn't take him long to recollect the female doctor who had come to him for an interview. He frowned.

Nancy Greenwood.

Yes, of course.

She had been on a training scheme in the picturesque cathedral city of Southbury, but there had been some kind of trouble and her trainer had rung Callum to ask if she could transfer to him. Dr Farrow, her trainer, had been reluctant to discuss her desire to change her training practice, other than to reassure Callum that she was an excellent doctor and that her reasons for wanting to move were personal, beyond her control and rather distressing.

That had been enough for Callum—he wasn't the kind of man to intrude, unasked, into someone's private life. He liked and respected Dr Farrow, both personally and professionally. An endorsement from such a man was all he needed to agree to see Dr Nancy Greenwood.

And the only fact which swam to the forefront of his memory of that meeting was that she had been so *small*! But, then, at an impressive six feet and three inches comparative lack of stature was something that Callum was well used to!

And young, he reminded himself suddenly. She had looked much too young to be a doctor. He remembered thinking that at the time and had seen that as a reflection on just how ancient *he* must be getting. Thirty-three next birthday—just where *did* the time go? he wondered fleetingly.

Jenny saw him frown. 'Her CV is on the top of that other pile if you want to look over it again before she arrives.'

'Thanks,' said Callum, but he was so engrossed in a leader from last week's *BMJ* that he didn't take in a word of Jenny's last sentence and the CV remained, sitting unread, on top of the pile.

The flame-red sports car slid to a halt outside Purbrook Surgery, drawing the usual mixture of admiring and envious glances.

Switching off the ignition to the accompaniment of interested stares, Nancy found herself wishing that she could trade it in for a more discreet and *ordinary* car— not one that risked alienating the patients because it looked so flashy! But she couldn't trade it in, not yet, anyway, because the car in question had been a present, and everyone knew that you should never look a gift horse in the mouth. . .

She got out of the car slowly, delaying walking into the surgery for as long as possible for she realised that her hands were still shaking like mad. The gold wedding band on her finger gleamed mockingly up at her as she tried to block this morning's row out of her memory and settle herself into a more receptive frame of mind for her first day as a trainee in general practice. A few deep breaths should help settle her equilibrium.

Nancy filled her lungs with air and expelled it slowly, vague memories from a distant yoga class coming to her aid as she pushed open the surgery door, determined that her face should not register her reaction to the ugly, biting taunts that she'd been forced to endure before she'd left for work this morning.

Shaking her head to dispel the all-too-vivid images of her husband's face distorted with a cold and untouchable anger, Nancy walked into the surgery—straight into the muted clatter of the main reception area.

Behind a desk sat the receptionists, some speaking into telephones as they made appointments and answered queries and others pulling patients' notes out of the grey filing cabinets which had mushroomed to fill all the available space behind them. A computer terminal hummed quietly in a corner and a fax machine began to spew out paper as a message came through.

One of the receptionists looked up questioningly at Nancy as she stood slightly hesitantly before the desk.

'Do you have an appointment?' she asked Nancy,

without preamble, her eyes flickering over her with interest.

Nancy shook her dark head. 'No, I haven't,' she began. 'You see, I—'

'I'm afraid that the doctor won't see you without an appointment,' said the woman automatically, though not quite as kindly as she might have done if Nancy hadn't been wearing a suit which probably cost as much as *her* entire month's salary!

Nancy, who had spent a sleepless night in the spare room and taken part in renewed hostilities at breakfast this morning, was not best pleased at being mistaken for a patient! Looking like a patient implied that you looked unwell or out of sorts. And that implication was a little too close for comfort!

'Do you always jump to conclusions?' she enquired mildly.

The receptionist bristled. 'I *beg* your pardon?' she queried frostily.

Nancy bit her lip. She really mustn't take all her impotent frustration out on a woman who was, after all, only doing her job. 'It's just that I'm Dr Hughes's new registrar, not a patient,' she explained helpfully. 'If you had simply asked whether you could help me, rather than whether or not I had an appointment. . .'

Her voice tailed off as the other woman glared at her, and she realised that she had put her foot right in it. Maybe Steve was right, she thought distractedly. Maybe she *was* impossible to live with.

'I have worked at this practice since it first opened ten years ago,' the receptionist informed her rather coldly, 'and I really think I am past the stage of being taught how to do my job properly—particularly by a newcomer!'

Nancy tried one more time. She managed a watery, apologetic smile. 'I'm terribly sorry. I honestly didn't mean to offend you,' she told the woman truthfully. 'It's just that at the moment I'm learning all about asking open-ended questions instead of closed questions, and I—'

'Please excuse me for a moment,' the woman said, looking slightly mollified as the telephone in front of her began to ring and she picked it up like a lifeline. 'Good morning!' she trilled brightly. 'Purbrook Surgery!'

Resisting the urge to ask someone else where she might find Dr Hughes—she didn't want to offend the receptionist still further—Nancy was forced to endure a tedious wait while the woman conducted her conversation.

Nancy waited until the receptionist had finished scribbling down what were obviously blood results from the local hospital and had replaced the receiver before fixing an inoffensive smile onto her face. 'I'm Dr Hughes's new GP registrar,' she said for the second time. 'Nancy Greenwood.'

The woman blinked. 'Registrar?' she queried blankly. '*Oh!* You mean you're the new trainee?'

Nancy shook her smooth, dark head. 'Not any more. We have a new name,' she answered with a rueful smile. 'I'm surprised that nobody bothered to tell you.'

'Oh, they probably did,' said the woman airily, 'but maybe you haven't worked in a doctors' surgery very much before—I'm afraid that the staff are much too busy with keeping everything running to learn new courtesy titles!'

Nancy was well practised in the art of keeping her face poker-straight. 'I'm sure you are,' she answered soothingly. 'And if you could just point me in the direction of Dr Hughes's consulting room I promise not to hold you up any longer.'

The woman hesitated, dying for the opportunity to witness Callum Hughes's reaction to this slimly built but rather opinionated young woman, but then the telephone shrilled into life again and she reluctantly indicated a big notice at the end of the corridor. 'Turn left at the end and just follow the signs to Dr Hughes's consulting room—you can't miss it!' she said quickly as she picked up the phone. 'Good morning! Purbrook Surgery!'

Nancy had to pick her way across the waiting room and every pair of eyes followed her—as they did all new arrivals—with an interest which bordered on the hypnotic.

There were very few people left, but it *was* almost eleven and consultations began at around eight-thirty. Nancy suspected that the waiting room would be full to bursting first thing in the morning.

The patients left were the usual mixed bunch—a hot-looking baby, grizzling in his frazzled mother's arms, a pale and sulky-looking boy of about ten who kicked listlessly at the leg of his chair and two people who appeared to be in the best of health, though sniffing loudly and intermittently. They looked ideal candidates for the diagnosis of heavy colds, though Nancy, but you never could tell. She knew that one of the cardinal rules of diagnosis was that you should never even think about making one before being cognisant with all the facts!

Nancy glanced around her as she walked towards the corridor where Dr Hughes had his office. Most of the waiting room, whilst decorated in the usual bland, pale shades, had a distinctively *homely* feel to it. Glossy magazines were stacked everywhere and brightly coloured toys were littered in one corner of the blue-grey carpet, where a small child was playing quite happily.

Nice to see that patient care had won over tidiness, thought Nancy approvingly. Though it *was* a bit like walking through a minefield, she decided with some amusement as her elegant navy court shoe only narrowly missed landing on a teddy bear's plump abdomen!

Dr Hughes's consulting room was at the far end of the corridor, and as she drew to a halt in front of it she noted that his brass name-plate was much longer than those of his two partners—for the simple reason that he seemed to have twice as many letters after his name as they did!

She rapped smartly on the door, and heard the equally smart response, 'Come!'

Nancy walked straight into the surgery and her veneer of composure was shattered like the breaking of a glass as she stared into the piercing green eyes of the broad-shouldered man, sitting behind the desk

CHAPTER TWO

WHEN Nancy Greenwood's name had been brought up earlier by Jenny, Callum's first thought had been that he remembered her only briefly and vaguely—but now he discovered he was wrong. Completely wrong.

Because when the door opened and the woman in the navy blue suit stood on its threshold, staring into his eyes, he was aware of nothing more than a bone-shaking *familiarity* about her. As if that earlier brief and apparently vague glimpse of her been enough to commit every line of her to everlasting and glorious memory.

She was as small as he remembered—a tiny, wee thing with soft, pale skin and clear brown eyes which were shaped like pebbles. Her hair was dark and shiny and clipped back rather severely from her face, though, in Callum's opinion, such restriction was unnecessary for he found he could imagine it, hanging in a glossy curtain to her shoulders, the way it had been when he'd interviewed her before.

He cleared his throat but, even so, his voice sounded even deeper than usual as he said, 'Come in, Dr Greenwood, though perhaps I'd better call you Nancy. You don't mind me calling you by your first name, do you?'

He raised his dark eyebrows enquiringly and Nancy shook her head automatically, both bemused and charmed by his obvious friendliness. At that precise

18

moment he could have called her anything he darned well pleased!

'I'm Callum Hughes,' he continued. 'And you must, of course, call me Callum. We're very informal here.'

'Yes, of course,' said Nancy, forcing herself to step forward on legs which threatened to tremble and wondering what it was that had *changed*.

Why did Dr Callum Hughes suddenly look like the most *vital* person she had ever seen? More real and more of a man than any man had a right to be? She found that her chest was tight as she looked at him, her breathing was rapid and shallow and her normally cool skin was feeling oddly clammy.

Had *he* changed? she wondered frantically. Or had she?

'How delightful to see you again,' Callum said, and extended a hand with strong, square fingers, experiencing such a disconcerting flare of disappointment as he noticed the shiny gold wedding band which circled her finger. Had she been wearing one before? he wondered.

Nancy allowed her hand to be firmly taken and shaken by his and tried to dampen the panicky feeling which was welling up inside her. Sucking in a deep breath, she forced herself to examine instead the man who seemed to be the cause of it.

From beneath the silky black cover of her eyelashes she allowed herself a brief but thorough scrutiny of the man with whom she would be working so closely for the next year.

Quite the most distinctive thing about him was his size, she decided immediately. He was well over six feet tall, with a powerfully muscular frame to match— more of a farmer's physique than a physician's, in

Nancy's opinion, with those strong, solid limbs and rugged features. He had a healthy looking energy about him that suggested a life spent mainly in the fresh air, rather than in the dark and smoky atmosphere of a nightclub.

And, although it was January, he was more tanned than last time she'd seen him. His skin was the deep, glowing colour produced by the sun on the ski-slopes, rather than the even tan of the dedicated sun-worshipper. His shoulders and arms certainly looked powerful enough to make light of the blackest of black runs, Nancy found herself thinking. Then she drew herself up, appalled at the forbidden paths her mind was taking. And she a married woman, too!

His deep voice interrupted her confused thoughts. 'Do sit down. I'll ring for coffee—'

'Oh, please don't, not just on my account,' Nancy protested.

'I'm not. It's on mine. And don't worry,' he added, with the glimmer of a smile, 'I won't feel at all inhibited or put out by the fact that you don't wish to join me—'

'Actually, I'd love some coffee,' said Nancy with sudden fervour, sinking into the chair he had indicated. She briefly closed her eyes and relaxed for the first time in days.

His eyes narrowed as he saw some of the tension ease out of her petite frame. Then he lifted the telephone on his desk to ask for coffee while Nancy cast her eyes quickly round his consulting room, wondering just how much she would be able to tell about Callum Hughes from his working environment.

His was a large, pale surgery with one huge window, the bottom half of which was glazed in frosted glass—

presumably to allow for patient privacy, Nancy decided. The top of the window allowed a view of the still-bare branches of trees, etched like broomsticks against the bright blue of the winter sky.

An old-fashioned wooden playpen, standing on one corner, was filled with a variety of toys, and on a brightly painted shelf above it was an impressive line of story-books for all different ages.

So he was considerate with children, too, thought Nancy, and a funny little lurch in her chest made her feel momentarily rather uncomfortable. . .

In one corner of the room stood a large fish tank full of rainbow-coloured shapes that darted around plants which swayed in the bubbles of the illuminated green water.

Callum had been watching her slow appraisal, and he waited until she had finished before saying with some amusement, 'And do you like my surgery, young Dr Greenwood?'

And then he wondered why he had said something as archaic as 'young'! Not something he normally did. So, was his subconscious, he asked himself critically, simply using a word designed to create some kind of distance between them? And, if so, was that really necessary at this stage?

Nancy had raised her eyebrows at his terminology and as their eyes met—his rueful, hers questioning— she suddenly burst out laughing, the spontaneous sound surprising both of them. To his astonishment, he found himself joining in.

'Young Dr Greenwood is fine, thank you very much,' she told him gravely. 'She adores your fish tank, and she's just itching to get into that playpen!'

'Did I sound very patronising?' he asked her seriously.

'No.' Nancy shook her glossy head thoughtfully. 'Not at all. You sounded—um—'

'Paternal?'

No, certainly *not* paternal! 'More avuncular,' she prevaricated, looking up gratefully as the door of the surgery opened and in walked one of the receptionists with a tray of coffee.

Callum immediately took the tray from the receptionist and cleared a space for it on his desk, before introducing them. 'Margaret, this is Nancy Greenwood, my new GP registrar.'

'Hello, Dr Greenwood,' said Margaret, giving Nancy a wide and friendly smile. 'I hope you'll be very happy during your time with us.'

'And why wouldn't she be?' queried Callum teasingly. 'We've a very happy practice.'

Margaret pulled an expressive he-must-be-joking sort of face, exclusively for Nancy's benefit, and left them to it.

Callum poured their coffee. 'How do you take it?' he asked, glancing up.'

'As it comes, please,' answered Nancy.

He handed her a steaming cup of black and unsugared coffee. 'No wonder you're so tiny,' he commented, as he added both cream and sugar to his own and offered her a biscuit.

And *he* didn't look at all bad on cream and sugar, Nancy found herself thinking, accepting a chocolate digestive as her stomach reminded her that she had rushed out of the house without eating any breakfast. Not an ounce of surplus fat anywhere, by the look of him. 'I'm strong for my size,' she defended.

'I'm sure you are.' Callum drank his coffee, then put down his empty cup and leaned back in his chair to look at her, trying to view her simply as a colleague—and a married colleague, to boot—instead of as a very attractive young woman. And it wasn't easy, he discovered, but he was at a loss to understand why. Not easy at all. 'So, where do we begin, Nancy Greenwood?' he asked gruffly.

'At the beginning?' she joked, wondering just what had made his green eyes grow so serious.

He nodded. 'OK. The beginning it is. We'd better begin with the district itself. How much to you know about Purbrook and the surrounding area?'

'Very little,' responded Nancy truthfully. 'We only moved into the area a month ago.'

We. The possessive word produced an inexplicably sour taste in Callum's mouth but he hoped that his reaction didn't show on his face. 'Yes, of course. You're married, aren't you?'

For some absurd reason the question caught her off guard. 'Yes, I am,' she answered in a low voice.

'And where do you live?

'In Tenterdon,' she answered, mentioning the picturesque market town which was approximately seven miles away.

He saw her look of bemusement and correctly interpreted it. 'Don't worry, Nancy,' he remarked drily, 'I'm not planning to turn up on your doorstep at odd times for surprise tutorials!'

'I'm very pleased to hear it!' Nancy blanched as she tried to imagine her husband's reaction if he *did*!

'Are you registered with a doctor in Tenterdon, or

were you planning to sign on with this practice?'

And risk Callum Hughes ministering to her if she should happen to fall ill? No fear! Nancy shook her head vigorously and stared steadily at the man in front of her. 'I wasn't going to, no. I'm perfectly happy where I am.'

Glad to divert his attention from the rather absorbing tawny-brown colour of her eyes, Callum slid open one of the desk drawers, took out a shiny clutch of leaflets and handed them to her.

'Then you won't have seen our practice brochure,' he explained, smiling as he pointed to the stick-like drawing on the front cover of a man covered in lurid red spots. 'We had a competition amongst all our younger patients for the cover design. The winner had all the delight of seeing her work in print—'

'Oh, but it's brilliant!' she enthused as she took the leaflet from him and stared down to admire the youthful artistry. 'Absolutely *brilliant!*'

His eyes crinkled at the corners. 'It *is* rather good, isn't it?'

'And can I keep this?'

'Of course you can. I sincerely hope you'll refer to it frequently!' Callum found himself smiling again as he watched her tuck the papers into a slim leather briefcase.

'Oh, day and night,' she promised, and clipped the case shut. 'It will never leave my side!'

Callum's eyes twinkled. In his opinion, a sense of humour applied to the working day wasn't just preferable but necessary. 'Most of the information given in the brochure about the practice is self-explanatory,' he told her. 'We are a semi-rural practice with a list size of just over five thousand patients. You really should become familiar with the geography and social class ecology of the practice area as soon as possible.'

'Right.' Nancy made a mental note to do that this very weekend.

'It's sensible to have a map of the practice with you at all times,' he continued, 'and to begin to become familiar with traffic flow during weekdays, and in particular at rush hours—although our rush hours are pretty small stuff compared to what inner-city doctors have to contend with.'

'I bought a map at the weekend,' said Nancy eagerly.

He smiled at her obvious enthusiasm. 'Good,' he murmured. 'As for the other members of the practice, I have two partners whom you'll meet later on. One is male and one female and I'll stagger the introductions as it's your first day, otherwise you won't remember anybody! We have a full complement of staff here, with a practice nurse, a district nurse, health visitor, midwife and community psychiatric nurse.'

Nancy nodded. 'As well as all the usual ancillary staff of receptionists, typists, a bookkeeper and filing clerk, I suppose?'

Callum smiled. 'For "ancillary" substitute "indispensable"! We would simply be unable to function without efficient receptionists who were firmly on our side. And we're very much a team here,' he added quickly.

Now was that an admonishment? Nancy wondered fleetingly. Had word reached him that within seconds of walking into the building she had clumsily been trying to explain an open-ended sentence to one of the receptionists and getting a rather stony-faced response?

But his face was resolutely non-judgemental, and Nancy inwardly reprimanded herself. She was getting paranoid, that was all. Too much criticism at home was making her normally strong sense of self-worth begin to crumble.

'And a team is what I want to be part of,' she told him firmly.

Her declaration seemed almost *defiant*, observed Callum thoughtfully. 'Good,' he said briskly. 'I've drawn up a timetable for you, but this is flexible and will change as you grow in confidence.' He pushed the neat chart across the desk at her, and Nancy began to study it.

'At first, you'll sit in on my surgeries and accompany me on my visits,' he told her. 'Then, when we both feel that you're ready to see patients on your own, we will give you small, selected surgeries. But remember that I'm always next door if you run into any problems.'

'I'll do my very best not to,' she told him with a smile.

'Good. Every day we'll have short tutorials on conditions we've encountered that day—influenza epidemics notwithstanding, of course! And once a week we'll have a longer tutorial on a subject which you will be able to choose—'

'Unless there's a topic which you feel I *ought* learn about?' she guessed.

Callum nodded, pleased at her perception. 'That's right. There is also an afternoon day-release course at St Saviour's Hospital on Wednesday afternoons especially for GP registrars, which I think you'll find very useful as well as providing an opportunity for you to meet some other people in the same boat as yourself.

'And I intend to go lightly with you when I'm on call.' He smiled. 'I'll make sure you get all the experience you need, but I'm aware that you'll need to study for your membership exam so if I'm up all night, working, I won't necessarily expect *you* to be!' His green eyes glittered as he watched her eyes widen. 'Any questions?'

Nancy gazed at him in a rather dazed fashion as the reality of just how much work she would have to do hit her. 'It sounds frantic,' she ventured.

Callum shook his head. 'It sounds more daunting than it actually is, but most of the job you'll learn as you go along. I often think that there is no finer tutor than experience, and in medicine this is especially true.'

'And presumably I'll be driven by a "need to know"?' prompted Nancy. 'Which will make me eager to learn?'

Callum nodded his dark head approvingly. 'You've obviously been reading up on the subject.'

'A bit.' Not as much as she would have liked, of course. Steve, her husband, had made sure of that. Nancy had wondered lately if he saw her career as some kind of threat. Sometimes he seemed almost *jealous* of the time she tried to put into her background reading.

He'd complained last night when she'd been curled up beside him on the sofa after dinner.

'*Must* you keep reading that?' he'd demanded.

Nancy had been bent over a textbook, trying her level best to get to grips with its particularly stodgy content, her dark, shiny hair falling in splendid disarray over her shoulders. She had calmly lifted her head to meet her husband's accusing stare head-on.

'I must spend a *little* time on my reading, Steve,' she'd observed, her voice determinedly conciliatory as she'd fruitlessly attempted to delay the row which would inevitably follow.

'But I thought that the whole *point* of you going into general practice was to stop working unsociable hours so that we could spend more time together!' He scowled.

Nancy laid her book down on her lap and tried to block out the whining tone in his voice. 'Actually, I thought the whole *point* of me going into general practice was to have an interesting and varied workload, while mixing with the whole community,' she corrected drily.

'And while I'm training I need to do plenty of reading, which I would have to do whichever speciality I'd chosen. I have an examination to take at the end of this year of training, and general practice is a busy job, you know, Steve.'

Steve looked at her disbelievingly. 'Well, *our* family GP used to spend three quarters of his time on the golf course!'

'And you think that's admirable, do you?' Nancy challenged, thinking how glad she was that such unprofessionalism would no longer be tolerated in these hardworking times.

'I think a lot of things,' he said with a glower, 'but I don't think that *you'd* care to hear any of them!'

He stood up and poured himself another three fingers of whisky, a practice which had been occurring much more frequently of late. 'And you can stop glaring at me like that!' he declared as he gazed unsteadily into her brown eyes.

'I wasn't glaring!'

'Oh, yes, you were! And I can tell you something else, Nancy Greenwood—that the amount of time you spend with your nose in a bloody textbook would drive a saint to drink!'

And Steve was certainly no saint. . .

*   *   *

Yet as Nancy looked across the desk at the approving face of her trainer she found herself thinking how wonderful it would be to have a partner who actually *supported* you, instead of undermining your determination to succeed.

But allowing her thoughts to drift in *that* direction would do no good whatsoever. There was absolutely no point in wishing for what you knew deep down you would never get. . .

Callum saw the apprehension that clouded her clear, brown eyes, but even if he hadn't correctly read it there it would have been apparent from her demeanour.

Her whole delicately boned frame had tensed, as though she were uncomfortable in her own body. Those narrow shoulders—*tiny* shoulders, Callum found himself thinking with an almost protective pang—were all bunched up beneath that navy blue suit she was wearing.

He looked at her clothes properly for the first time.

Callum was not the kind of person who was particularly interested in the clothes that women wore. And whilst the man in him could recognise and acknowledge the sexual allure of a woman clad in a shimmering and clinging gown—with all its accompanying glitz—he nevertheless preferred women to look more natural. He liked the kind of woman who would climb out of bed and into an old pair of jeans to walk for miles, before tackling a hearty breakfast.

He sighed. Bit of a shortage of those women, really. And—here his eyes flickered to Nancy's structured navy jacket—this woman wouldn't fit into that category either. Not with a suit that must have cost most of a month's salary. Callum couldn't have named a dress designer to save his life, but he was enough of an aesthete to recognise and appreciate the superb cut of the finely woven material and the way it moulded itself so beautifully to the curving lines of her body.

Their eyes met, and something in his expression made Nancy's cheeks grow faintly pink.

Callum shook his head impatiently. For God's *sake*, man, he told himself, she was his trainee and she was *married* so he'd better stop ogling her right now!

He put on his professional smile, with a brisk professional tone to match. 'We've a few minutes to spare so I'll give you a quick guided tour of the health centre. Then we'd better get a couple of these visits out of the way before lunch,' he said brusquely.

He stood up, and immediately dominated the surgery. 'I tend to buy a sandwich and eat it in between visits. I hope that's OK with you? That way we can talk in the car on the way.'

'Right,' gulped Nancy, wondering what had prompted his sudden change of disposition.

'Then let's go,' he said in a clipped voice, and led the way out of the surgery.

Callum's bad mood lasted only as long as it took them to reach their first visit. Nancy couldn't help noticing that he was politeness personified when it came to dealing with patients.

The visits which were logged in his book were fairly straightforward. First up was a new baby to check over, who had just arrived home from hospital.

The family lived in a small house on one of Purbrook's two housing estates, and it seemed completely swamped by baby equipment. There were numerous toys and giant packets of nappies, as well as an enormous pram, a pushchair and a car seat. And

Nancy only just narrowly avoided tripping over a baby-walker!

Mrs Morris, the new mother, seemed rather stupefied by the whole experience, although Daniel, her baby, glugged away happily at her breast. 'I can't take it all in,' she murmured. 'There just seems to be so much which is new!'

'Baby shock,' said Callum with a grin as he straightened up from listening to Daniel's chest. 'It happens to all new mums, Mrs Morris, but, rest assured, you have a fine, bouncing baby. Oh, and I'm very glad to see you're breast-feeding!'

Mrs Morris cast a rueful eye around the cramped sitting room. 'I simply wouldn't have had *room* for a steriliser and all the bottles, even if I'd wanted to!' she told them. 'We're hoping to move to a cottage on the outskirts of Purbrook soon. It's very basic but there's room to build on—my husband is a builder, you know—and it's got a *huge* garden!'

'Plenty of room for young Daniel to run around, then,' said Callum, with an approving nod.

'That was the general idea,' agreed Mrs Morris, staring lovingly down at her baby's bald head.

Their next port of call was to a small, sheltered housing complex for the elderly. 'I want to pop in on an old lady named Ethel Waters and take her blood pressure—it's been all over the place lately,' explained Callum, as the car drew up in the well-tended grounds.

'Can't she get out to the surgery, then?' queried Nancy.

He pulled a face. 'She *can*, but she's fairly immobile due to arthritis. I tend to think that it's not much of an outing for a lady in pain to have to get down to the doctor's surgery!'

Nancy smiled with delight at his level of understanding and consideration. 'That's very sweet of you,' she told him.

'Why, thank you, Nancy,' he responded, but the mock gravity in his voice couldn't disguise the unaccountable pleasure he took in her praise.

They were drinking a cup of tea with the old lady, whose blood pressure was reassuringly low, when Callum's bleeper went off.

'May I use your telephone, please, Mrs Waters?' he enquired putting his empty teacup down in the saucer.

'Course you can, Doctor!'

The call was urgent, and they drove to it as quickly as the law would allow. 'What's up?' asked Nancy, as he roared past a picturesque grey church.

'An elderly lady is wandering around her garden naked?' he replied calmly.

'*Who?*' cried Nancy in alarm.

'Mrs Dolly Anderson,' said Callum. 'She's an elderly patient with dementia, and she copes well enough with the assistance of the home help and Meals-on-Wheels.'

'And has she ever done anything like this before?' asked Nancy.

'Never.'

'Then I wonder what's changed,' said Nancy thoughtfully.

Callum's eyes gleamed at her perceptiveness. 'Precisely,' he observed, his voice equally thoughtful.

Their answer came soon enough. Once Mrs Anderson had been gently persuaded into the house and into a dressing-gown Callum was able to assess his patient properly.

Only when he had concluded his examination did Callum turn to Nancy. 'Mrs Anderson is wheezy and has a slight cough and temperature. Do you want to have a shot at a diagnosis?'

'Could it be a chest infection?' she asked hesitantly. 'Which would make her more than usually confused?'

He nodded. 'I think so. I'm going to admit her to the medical ward at St Saviour's—that's if they have a bed!'

They did, although Callum had to sweet-talk the admitting team into allocating them one.

'Hospital beds are like gold dust these days,' he complained as he talked Nancy through the admission procedure, before setting off for the surgery.

A moment's peace and quiet seemed equally elusive, thought Nancy with a touch of amusement.

'Coping OK so far?' he asked her, as they buckled themselves back into the car.

'So far,' she grinned, wondering what had caused his grumpiness earlier but then dismissing the thought because when he was being sunny and helpful like this she could have stuck to his side like glue all day.

CHAPTER THREE

THE house was in darkness, and it was seven forty-five
before Nancy finally fumbled around in her briefcase
for her house keys. She pushed open the front door of
the modern glass and steel townhouse she called home
and listened for the sound of her husband.

Silence.

She felt a moment's disloyalty for the rush of relief
she experienced as she closed the door behind her and
switched on the light.

'Steve?' she called, more out of habit than anything
else, as a soft light illuminated the spacious hall.

She checked the answerphone but there were no messages so she went upstairs and changed out of the rather
formal navy suit, which Steve had bought for her, into
jeans and a big, floppy sweater. Then she came back
down, made some tea and sat at the kitchen table, drinking it, while she decided whether it was worth cooking
supper.

Steve was so unpredictable, that was the trouble.
Sometimes—usually when she had pulled all the stops
out with an exotic new recipe and bought candles and
flowers—he would moan that he had eaten an enormous
business lunch and that he simply wasn't hungry.

At other times—and this always seemed to coincide
with Nancy being too dog-tired from working to even
think about food—he would complain that she never
seemed able to provide the same creature comforts as

the wives of his partners. Women who, from Steve's glowing descriptions, seemed to embody all the qualities which made up the ideal wife. They cooked, they cleaned, they sewed and they gardened, and—apparently—achieved a blissful state of contentment from all these activities.

In other words, thought Nancy, trying to subdue a trace of bitterness as she slipped at her tea, wives without children who did no work outside the home.

She yawned as she thought back over her first afternoon in practice. It had been hard work. Non-stop, in fact. After visits and a baby clinic, which had run over time, they'd had what had seemed like an endless evening surgery, composed mostly of patients complaining of sore throats.

Then the medical registrar from St Saviour's had rung to say that a chest X-ray on Mrs Anderson had confirmed Nancy's and Callum's diagnosis of a chest infection, and that they were going to start her on a regime of intravenous antibiotics.

It was after one of the receptionists had rung through to ask if Callum could squeeze an extra patient onto the end of his already long evening surgery that Nancy had turned on him and said, half in amusement and half in exasperation, 'Is it always like this?'

He'd looked up from scrubbing his hands, which the last patient—a baby—had been sick over. 'Like what?'

'*Busy!*'

'*Busy?*' He'd pulled an expressive face as he'd dried his hands on a paper towel and thought back to how it had been just before Christmas. 'This is a doddle, Nancy. Just you wait until a flu bug sweeps the community and *then* you'll understand the meaning of busy!'

'I can't wait,' Nancy had said faintly, but his remark had brought home to her that, contrary to what their hospital colleagues might have imagined, general practice was certainly not a relaxed way to idle away the day!

Nancy leaned her elbows dreamily on the table as her mind drifted over everything they had accomplished during that busy afternoon. Because, despite the unaccustomedly frantic pace, it had also been one of the most interesting days of her medical career so far.

Or was that simply because Callum Hughes was such an astute and sympathetic teacher. . .?

She opened up the textbook which Callum had loaned her and began to read about red eye in general practice, becoming so engrossed in the subject that she didn't hear the front door open and close—didn't hear anything, in fact, until a slight movement arrested her attention and she looked up to find Steve standing in the doorway, watching her.

'Hello,' said Nancy, her eyes sweeping over his face in an attempt to try and gauge what kind of mood he was in.

His eyes were glittering hectically as he stared at the book she was reading and then let his gaze move slowly around the kitchen. 'And what's for supper?' he asked carefully, in an oddly controlled voice which immediately told Nancy that he had been drinking, even if she hadn't been able to smell it on his breath from the other side of the kitchen.

Seeing from the wall clock that it was now gone nine, she closed the textbook and smiled brightly, 'To be honest, I hadn't really given it a thought—'

'I can see *that*!' he sneered, opening the fridge door

and taking out a bottle of white wine. 'Too busy with your precious textbooks again.'

'But, Steve, you weren't even at *home*,' she said, putting on her most reasonable voice, 'so what was the point of preparing something when I wasn't even sure you'd want it?'

'I called you earlier,' he responded icily, as he began to twist the corkscrew into the bottle, 'and you were out.'

'But there were no messages on the answerphone!' Nancy pointed out in confusion. 'I looked!'

Steve's eyes glittered dangerously. 'So you've been checking up on me, have you?'

'No,' answered Nancy steadily. 'Why should I want to do that?'

He shrugged. 'You tell me,' came the slightly threatening reply.

His handsome face looked ugly—bloated and red with drink—and Nancy was aware that she was handling this all wrong and that by sounding so defensive it was giving him the opportunity to attack her.

'Are you hungry?' she asked calmly.

'Not for food,' came the unsteady reply, and his eyes focussed blearily on her breasts. 'Why d'you have to wear that horrible sloppy jumper?' he grumbled, as he eased the cork out of the bottle with a resounding pop. 'Hides all your assets.'

Nancy felt ill, torn between telling Steve that he had already drunk quite enough and keeping quiet about it. She knew that if he continued to drink at the same rate at least he wouldn't start pawing at her.

As a doctor she knew what her advice *should* be, and as a wife she knew that she wasn't going to give it.

She rose to her feet, keeping her distance. 'Shall I

make you an omelette? Or there's some frozen curry in the freezer. I could microwave that.'

Steve splashed some wine into a large glass and slugged half of it back. 'If you want,' he mumbled. 'I'm going to watch TV.'

Nancy watched him pick up the bottle and glass and wander towards the sitting room. Guilt, mixed with an overwhelming sense of relief, washed over her until an immense sadness obliterated everything.

Whatever had happened to him?

To her?

To *them*?

Nancy frowned as she pulled open the freezer door, her mind flitting back to when they had met—when the world had seemed a much less complicated place.

To the worldly Steve, the bookish Nancy had seemed like a creature from another planet. He'd never met a woman who was more interested in studying than in buying clothes or going out.

As an account executive of a successful regional advertising agency, Steve had had all the accoutrements of success achieved at an early age—the fast cars, the designer clothes and the luxurious holidays in far-flung corners of the globe, as well as the slightly spoilt air of cynical detachment, which seemed to fascinate members of the opposite sex. Women had spent their lives flinging themselves at him.

But Nancy didn't fling herself at him—in fact, she'd scarcely noticed him. It was a new and heady experience for the worldly Steven Greenwood, and he'd pursued her with a flattering and ardent dedication until at last she'd agreed to go out with him.

Steve's world had been a very different world to the

one which Nancy had been used to inhabiting, and their very differences had been what at first had attracted them to each other. It had been exciting to be with a man who hadn't always had his head in a book—who had done wild, crazy things on impulse, instead of writing essays.

But at the back of her mind Nancy had suspected that the relationship had had no solid footing to bolster up the purely physical appeal which had existed between them. More than once she had tentatively broached the subject of their incompatibility with Steve, but he had kissed her doubts away and eventually taken her to bed.

Nancy's upbringing had been a conventional one—you saved your virginity for the man you loved and would marry. She had never questioned this point of view and it had seemed to be satisfactorily backed up by her parents' long and happy marriage. So that when, soon after he had taken her to bed for the first time, Steve had asked to marry her she had turned to him happily and said yes.

So just how could dreams die and hope be eroded after less than two years together? she wondered sadly as she took a couple of plates down from the cupboard.

Fifteen minutes later she carried a steaming tray into the sitting room. On it were two delicious platefuls of chicken bhuna and saffron rice, with accompanying naan and a side-salad. She had even put a glass on the tray. She would join Steve for a drink, and that way he would drink less himself. They would eat a delicious meal in front of the fire and she would let him watch the video of *his* choice, which usually meant a film with a cast composed entirely of men!

Though, come to think of it, mused Nancy wryly as

she padded through from the kitchen, carefully balancing the tray, he usually *did* watch the video of his choice, anyway!

Nancy came to a halt in the doorway.

On the sofa, sprawled out with all the abandonment of a sleeping toddler, lay her husband. The remote control lay like a prayer-book on his chest, even as the television droned on, ignored, in the corner. The wine bottle was already empty.

Nancy put the tray down and went to wake him.

'Steve,' she called softly, and shook him gently by the shoulder.

For answer he simply expelled some sour breath from his mouth and sucked in a huge, shuddering breath.

Nancy was no stranger to this routine.

With a sigh, she made him comfortable and removed his shoes and socks, then covered him up with a spare blanket kept in the cupboard underneath the stairs. Then she carried the tray back to the kitchen and binned its contents.

Only then, after a final check, did she turn off the television, snap off the sitting-room light and leave her husband, snoring, in the darkness.

The first day back after a holiday was always exhausting but today had been especially wearing, and Callum did something he hadn't done for years.

He went to the pub on the way home from work.

Purbrook had several pubs, but in Callum's opinion the Crown served the best beer—and was also the closest to his sprawling thatched cottage which overlooked the surrounding fields. At weekends he would occasionally pop in for a pint, and had been known to bring girlfriends in to sample some of the landlady's famous steak and ale pies.

The pub was low-ceilinged and beamed, with a real fire in the corner. Pewter mugs, belonging to regular customers, hung above the bar and gleamed in a dull, beaten-silver row.

Tom Watts had been the landlord of the Crown for longer than most people could remember, and he beamed with delight as Callum stooped his head to pass underneath the low doorway and went to stand at the bar.

'Evening, Doctor.' He smiled proudly. It added a certain cachet if one of the local doctors happened to drink in *your* establishment! 'Pint of the usual, is it?'

'Please.' Callum nodded. He watched while Tom carefully poured the drink, then took the foaming tankard with a grateful smile.

Several of his patients were dotted around the pub but they paid him no heed, other than to greet him. And that was just the way Callum liked it. As a family doctor working in a semi-rural area privacy was essential, and he appreciated the fact that most of his patients realised that—out of hours—he liked to be left alone!

He'd almost invited Nancy Greenwood to join him for a drink, but something had stopped him from asking her at the last minute. Which was pretty ridiculous, when you thought about it. Women these days—especially career women, in Callum's experience—demanded that they be treated equally. And rightly so!

If Nancy had been a *male* colleague he would have suggested a drink, without giving it a second thought. So why hadn't he? Because she was a woman? Was that the reason for his reluctance? But Callum had been working quite happily with women for years.

Because she was married? Was that closer to the truth, then? Because, against his will, he had found her utterly captivating? Callum rubbed his square jaw and felt the rasping of new beard beneath his fingers. He sincerely hoped that was not going to be the case.

Infatuation was nothing more than an inconvenience, especially if it stood no chance of ever being reciprocated. And Callum was enough of a moralist and a traditionalist to be appalled at the thought of a married woman ever straying.

He drank his pint slowly and refused all offers of a refill. 'No, thanks, Tom,' he said, in his deep, resonant voice. 'You wouldn't thank me if you came into my surgery tomorrow morning and I was all grouchy and headachy from drinking too much, now would you?'

Tom smiled. He simply couldn't imagine the scenario of a hungover Dr Hughes! In the seven years since Dr Hughes had come to practice in Purbrook he had looked after Tom's family brilliantly. It had been Dr Hughes who had noticed that Tom's and Rowena's son, Robin, had been failing to thrive—even before his mother did. And it had been Dr Hughes who had rung up a pal at London's biggest paediatric hospital for an urgent appointment.

Now Robin was doing as well as any other boy his age, and all thanks to the good doctor.

'Not like you to call in after work, Doctor,' Tom ventured.

'Well, you know what they say about a holiday,' responded Callum, draining the last of his beer. 'You need another one to recover from it!'

'Sure I can't tempt you with some of Rowena's steak and kidney pud?'

Callum was tempted, but for no more than a moment. Rowena's meals were legendary but colossal, and he had just spent a fortnight eating food that was far richer than his usual fare. He was also a doctor who firmly adhered to what he taught his patients. Accordingly, he ate and drank moderately most of the time, abhorred smoking and took exercise almost daily. But hoped that he wasn't *too* sanctimonious about his lifestyle!

'No, thanks, Tom,' said Callum, putting his empty tankard on the counter. 'I'll grab something at home. I've a lot to catch up on—and a new doctor under my wing, who's learning all about general practice. So, if you make an appointment to see me with a fairly straightforward problem, you might just get the new doctor.'

Tom nodded. 'Good bloke, is he?'

'She,' Callum corrected, thinking of pale skin, clear brown eyes and a tiny frame dressed much too severely in stark designer clothes. 'The new doctor is a she.'

'Is she now?' asked Tom, his eyes lighting up with interest, but Callum elaborated no further and said goodnight.

Tom watched him leave, wondering why—not for the first time—the good doctor had never married.

And most surprisingly, Callum found himself asking the very same question as he let himself into the impractical, draughty and thoroughly beautiful thatched cottage he had bought and renovated when he had first arrived in Purbrook.

Most family doctors of his age had a wife, but Callum often suspected that some of his colleagues' marriages were precipitated by the desire to have someone answer the phone for them and provide warm meals, rather than because they had found their true soul-mates.

Callum was the product of a successful marriage which had also been a love match and, consequently, he was unwilling to settle for anything less than the best. And a close brush with matrimony in his twenties had made him even more wary of commitment.

Indeed, sometimes he suspected that his expectations were too high to ever be realised, and that he might be consigning himself to a solitary future. But isolation posed less worry to him than failure in a relationship, particularly if that relationship involved children. For Callum had been a doctor for long enough to understand the far-reaching repercussions of divorce on family life.

At home there was a message on his answerphone, asking him to ring Helen. He knitted his dark eyebrows together, and it took a moment for him to remember that she was the rather luscious actress he had met at his younger brother's Christmas party. Blonde, attractive and sunny in nature, she had been appearing in panto on the south coast and had promised to get in touch once the run had ended.

Callum hesitated as he recalled a pale and fluffy dress which had clung to an outrageously curved body. Yes, he *would* ring her, he decided—but not tonight!

Tonight he would write down a list of topics which his new GP registrar might wish to discuss with him.

CHAPTER FOUR

NANCY awoke with a splitting headache and the dull ache of hunger gnawing away at the pit of her stomach. She turned to stare at the space beside her on the bed, and again felt relief and guilt in equal measures on discovering that it was empty.

She showered and dressed, before going downstairs. She felt much too vulnerable to face her husband wearing nothing but a pair of cotton-brushed pyjamas which fell in soft folds against her bare skin.

Steve was sleeping just where she had left him, still snoring—his mouth open and moistly slack—sucking in great shuddering breaths of air. She went into the kitchen, made a pot of strong, black coffee and poured him a vast mugful, before attempting to shake him awake.

'Go *away*!' he mumbled, and turned his head into one of the cushions.

'Steve, I'm not going anywhere,' she told him patiently, even though the stale smell of alcohol made her want to gag. 'It's eight o'clock in the morning, and I have to leave for surgery in five minutes. You, meanwhile, have a client meeting booked for ten-thirty so I suggest you drink this and dive into the shower.' She bent and loudly crashed the coffee-mug onto the table next to the sofa. 'Pronto!'

An eyelid flickered open and a bloodshot blue eye glowered at her. 'What time is it?' he mumbled.

'Eight o'clock,' Nancy repeated patiently.

Steve sat bolt upright, then groaned as he sank back again. 'Why the hell didn't you wake me?'

'I just have!'

'I meant last *night*.'

'Because,' answered Nancy very coolly, 'you were unrousable, that's why—but, then, that *is* what generally happens when you consume a bottle of wine within twenty minutes of opening it, particularly if you've already been drinking.'

Steve levered himself up onto an elbow and winced. 'Ooh! Just listen to little Miss Goody Two-Shoes!' he mocked. 'Some people just doesn't know how to live!'

It briefly crossed Nancy's mind that her idea of living didn't involve getting drunk and then passing out cold on the sofa, but she didn't feel it a prudent time to say so. She glanced at her watch. 'I have to go.'

Steve's eyes flickered to the swell of her breasts beneath the crisp green shirt she wore. 'Must you?' he said slowly and very deliberately.

Nancy didn't need to look at the opaque narrowing of his eyes to know exactly what he was getting at. The rough edge to his voice told its own story, and she was horrified at the shudder of revulsion that automatically prickled its way up her spine. She uttered a silent prayer that Steve hadn't noticed. 'Yes, I must. I don't want to be late. I'll see you tonight.'

And before he could attempt to kiss her or pull her into his arms she picked up her briefcase and slammed her way out of the front door.

The roads were still slippery and Nancy drove extra-carefully as she negotiated her way through the narrow country lanes in her little red sports car. She saw the silver-white glittering of frost which covered the ploughed earth and made the bare fields look like huge chunks of iced ginger cake. Magical, she thought, drinking in the view and putting Steve out of her mind completely.

She arrived in the doctors' car park at exactly the same time as Callum, and the sight of his slow smile unexpectedly had her grating her gears in the most dreadful display of parking she'd exhibited since she was a learner driver!

She gritted her teeth with frustration and climbed with difficulty out of the low car, wishing that he wasn't politely holding the door open for her since it was very difficult to manoeuvre her way out of it with any degree of grace. Not with a pencil-slim skirt on, anyway.

'Nice car,' he commented.

'It looks nice,' came her dry response as she locked it, 'but it's highly impractical—it eats petrol and attracts vandals. Also, every time I stop at a traffic light some man always sees it as a personal challenge to race me.'

'Then why not change it?' suggested Callum mildly.

Nancy only just stopped herself from coming out with a very rude comment indeed. 'Because it was a present from my husband,' she told him, more wearily than she knew. 'He paid a lot of money for it, and he's always telling me how much they appreciate in value. He'd be mortified if I changed it.'

Which gave Callum a surprising and rather disturbing insight into the dynamics of Nancy's relationship with her husband. 'I see,' he said neutrally, reminding himself that what went on between his trainee and her husband was none of his damned business.

Side by side they walked into the health centre, where

patients had already begun to congregate in the waiting room.

Callum bent over the desk to ask one of the receptionists to bring coffee down to the surgery, then turned to Nancy. 'Have you eaten anything this morning?'

She shook her head. She hadn't last night, either. Hence the gnawing feeling in her stomach, that slight light-headedness. 'No.'

'You didn't yesterday,' he pointed out with a frown.

'Ten out of ten for observation,' came her dry response, even though she knew that he was making a reasonable point.

'No wonder you're so pale. A very bad habit to get into, Nancy,' he commented sternly. 'Not eating breakfast.'

Jenny, the practice manager, who had been hovering nearby, pricked up her ears at this. 'That's a bit rich,' she chortled, and winked at Nancy. 'Coming from the man who gets the receptionist to buy him Danish pastries for breakfast!'

'That's different,' he demurred, blithely ignoring their outraged expressions. 'Women get into this stupid thing of counting calories—'

'I am *not* counting calories,' retorted Nancy, between gritted teeth. 'I simply didn't have the time to eat breakfast this morning, that's all.'

Callum stilled as he heard her barely stifled impatience. Of course. How completely dense of him! No wonder she didn't have time. He'd glanced over her CV last night and discovered that she'd only been married eighteen months. She and her husband, like all newlyweds, probably missed lots of meals, preferring to make love instead. A muscle flickered in his tanned cheek and he made the decision to ring Helen that very evening.

No, he couldn't, not tonight—tonight was his night on call for the practice. Well, tomorrow night, then.

Definitely.

'I'll bring you both something down,' said Jenny, looking from one to the other as she picked up something of the tension in the air.

Callum nodded. 'Thanks, Jenny! Now, let's go,' he said curtly to Nancy, and led the way through the waiting room to his surgery.

On his desk were the notes of all the patients booked in to see him, and Callum picked them up and quickly scanned through them.

'A lot of these visits are follow-ups, and there are quite a few of them because of my holiday,' he told her. 'Blood-pressure checks and repeat prescriptions, mainly—and the latter must be thoroughly reassessed. I never hand out prescriptions, willy-nilly, and I hope that you won't, either.'

'No, of course not,' said Nancy, nodding her head with enthusiasm as she warmed to his obvious dedication.

'Also, there will doubtless be a few conditions among these which should have been investigated days ago and weren't,' he continued.

'How come?' asked Nancy, with interest.

'Oh, patients of mine who are disinclined to see one of the other partners while I'm on holiday. They hang on and hang on until I get back, by which time the condition has either cleared up by itself or become far more serious than if it had been brought to our attention earlier.'

'Such devotion,' teased Nancy, and twisted a stray strand of dark hair round and round her finger. 'Is touching.'

Callum found his eyes unwillingly drawn to the simple gesture, and his heart rapidly began to pick up speed. Angry with his autonomic nervous system for its odd and strong response to this woman, Callum jabbed his finger on the button of the intercom that stood on his desk to relay messages to the waiting room.

'Mr Allen to see Dr Hughes,' he growled into the intercom, and something forbidding in his green eyes made Nancy sit there mute and uncomfortable while they waited for the patient to arrive.

Peter Allen was a forty-seven-year-old bus inspector, slightly overweight and very red in the face. He was puffing a little as he sat down in front of Callum, who waited until the patient had settled himself before he said, 'So, what brings you here today, Mr Allen?'

'It's these headaches, Doctor,' puffed Mr Allen.

'What kind of headaches?'

'Oh, it's nothing new! I've always suffered from them, even as a teenager—it's something you just get used to! I usually take something that the chemist gives me, which seems to work well enough. But over the last couple of months they've got worse. And they seem to come more often.' He looked directly into Callum's eyes. 'Could it be my blood pressure, do you think, Doctor?'

Callum nodded. 'That is one possibility, yes. And I would like to take your blood pressure, as a matter of course.'

'What, now?' demanded Mr Allen.

He looked alarmed as he asked the question, thought

Nancy, as if Callum had suggested emergency surgery instead of a relatively simple procedure! But she knew that what frightened Mr Allen was the fear that Callum might suddenly find something terribly wrong with him. Many patients had these fears—it sometimes made them resist the most simple of procedures.

'If you don't mind. Try not to worry—it'll only take a second.' Callum smiled encouragingly as he reached across the desk for his sphygmomanometer, and the patient unbuttoned his shirtsleeve and rolled it up beyond the elbow.

'So, have there been any major changes in your life recently?' asked Callum conversationally, as he wrapped the cuff around Mr Allen's arm. 'Around about the time when your headaches got worse, perhaps?'

Mr Allen pulled a face as Callum put the stethoscope in his ears and pumped up the cuff. 'I got promoted, actually, Doctor. The wife's very pleased.'

'I expect she must be,' murmured Callum automatically, his attention on the slowly falling level of mercury and the sudden slow pulsing as systolic and diastolic were reached. He straightened and waited until Mr Allen had rolled his shirtsleeve back again before he spoke.

'Your blood pressure *is* a little on the high side—'

'I *knew* it!' said the patient triumphantly, his fears of having it confirmed now forgotten.

'But blood pressure is like weight, and can vary tremendously under different circumstances,' continued Callum in measured tones. 'For example, you're probably slightly nervous at having to come and see me, and that could be partly responsible for the high reading today. I think that the best solution would be to take a number of readings over a period of time and see what the average figure is.'

'Is it serious, Doctor?' demanded Mr Allen.

'Not serious enough to require treatment at the moment—put it like that,' said Callum reassuringly. 'And manageable enough for you to be able to do something about it yourself.'

'With tablets, you mean?'

Callum shook his dark head. 'Not with tablets, no. But I can suggest some simple changes that can make a dramatic difference to your health.'

'Go on,' said Mr Allen, with undisguised interest.

He wasn't the only one. Nancy sat on the edge of her seat, too, and listened to Callum explain in wonderfully lucid terms just how weight loss and exercise and giving up smoking and moderation were things that *everyone* could do to improve their health.

And he did it with such gentle passion that he soon had Mr Allen nodding with conviction. He was looking positively *excited* as he left the surgery with a diet sheet and various booklets about healthy living clutched tightly in his calloused hands, having promised to follow Callum's advice to the letter.

'*Well...*' said Nancy slowly, after the door had closed behind him.

Callum looked up from the notes he was making. 'Well, what?'

'That was *very* impressive!'

He looked pleased. 'Really?'

'Mmm, really!' Nancy nodded. 'I could have saved myself six years of medical school if I'd heard that first!' She laughed. 'You almost had me vowing to decrease my intake of chocolate!'

Her spontaneous laughter liberated something in him, and Callum pursed his lips disbelievingly as his eyes flicked irresistibly over her tiny frame. 'Och, you're not telling me that a wee thing like you eats chocolate?'

'*Eats* chocolate?' she joked. 'This wee thing would live and breathe it if she could!' And as she found herself repeating the unfamiliar word he'd used a question suddenly formed itself in her mind, and she asked it, without thinking. 'You're Scottish, are you, Callum?'

It was not normally the kind of thing he would have talked about in surgery. If the question had been asked by anyone else he might have answered warily, but he found his response to this woman oddly instinctive. 'Partly. My mother is Scottish.' He smiled, and his green eyes crinkled at the corners as he spoke. 'But she fell in love with, and married, an Englishman, and went to live with him in Cornwall. Which is about as far away from Scotland as you can get, when you think about it! But, naturally, I have some of her phrases—'

'Which you don't often use?' guessed Nancy.

'Not often, no,' came his thoughtful reply, wondering why he should have suddenly come out with the comfortable words and inflections of his upbringing. 'And what about you?' he queried casually. 'Which part of the world do you hail from, Nancy Greenwood?'

'From just outside a place called Deal,' she told him, with a smile. 'In Kent.'

He nodded. He had heard of the small seaside town near Canterbury, naturally, but had never been there. 'Brothers and sisters?' he enquired.

She shook her dark head. 'No. Just me. An only child—or a *fille unique*, as the French say, which sounds infinitely more flattering! My parents are both doctors—

my mothers is much more high-powered than my father. I sometimes used to think that she didn't mean to have *any* children, really—'

'But then you came along?' he interposed gently, wondering if she was aware just how vulnerable and very young that last statement made her sound.

She saw what he was driving at, and sprang immediately to her parents' defence. 'Oh, I had a very happy childhood,' she told him.

'But both parents worked full time?'

'That's right—well, more than full time, really—you know what it's like for doctors. But we always had very nice au pairs. . . Well, nearly always. . .' She shrugged, and her voice tailed off as she realised that Callum had somehow managed to elicit the most honest description of her childhood that she had ever given.

And something in the soft understanding which tinted his eyes a deep, dark green made her long to tell him more. 'It *could* be lonely sometimes,' she admitted painfully, 'but it was a comfortable childhood. I had the best education and the best books that money could buy. I never wanted for anything.'

Except closeness, Callum thought. And time. He leaned back in the chair and watched her, thinking how their conversation seemed to have shifted so easily into an intimate one. Reluctantly, he dragged his mind back to what they were *supposed* to be talking about. He cleared his throat. 'So, what thoughts do you have about Mr Allen's future, Nancy?'

It was an effort for Nancy to force her mind back to the present, too, and she was wondering just who he was talking about when she remembered that Mr Allen was the name of the patient with high blood pressure who had just been in!

What on earth had she been *thinking*? She was supposed to be discussing hypertension, not baring her soul to a man she hardly knew—and not a friend, either, but someone who was in a position of authority. She was his subordinate, for heaven's sake!

She stared deep into his grass-green eyes, as if seeking inspiration, while she attempted to put her muddled thoughts into some semblance of order. She racked her brains to recall what impressions she had gauged from the patient, and a few salient facts came to her rescue.

'Um—as you said, single blood pressure readings are notoriously unreliable,' she ventured, encouraged by the enthusiastic nodding of his head.

'Yes, they are,' he agreed. 'So what will we do?'

'Um—an average of three readings, taken under standard conditions, is a significantly more reliable indicator.'

'Good,' he said, pleased. 'And at what level should blood pressure be treated?'

She had exhausted her supply of facts about hypertension, and she suspected that he was the kind of man who would prefer honesty to guesswork so she shrugged her narrow shoulders and looked at him apologetically.

'I don't know,' she answered simply.

He smiled. 'Good. Very good.'

'*Good?*' she squeaked.

'Mmm. You wouldn't believe how many doctors are afraid to admit that they don't know something.'

'How come?' she asked. 'Is it pride? Doesn't a lack of knowledge imply ignorance?'

'Perhaps. Maybe it's got something to do with the

fact that doctors are supposed to have an answer for everything—'

'And do you?' she interrupted, her eyes glinting with mischief. 'Have an answer for everything, Callum?'

It was meant to be a light-hearted remark but it came out all wrong as a sort of gurgling, throaty, sexy little aside, and she saw him frown in response.

'I can certainly advise you on the current treatment for hypertension,' he said coldly. 'A recent study has shown that treatment is effective at diastolic readings above 110 mmHg. At present, research is continuing into the effectiveness of treatment in the diastolic range of 100–110Hg.' The line of his mouth was distinctly forbidding. 'Evidence strongly suggests that treatment is effective in reducing morbidity and mortality for people whose blood pressure is in this range, but so far it isn't conclusive. I can loan you a couple of books, if you want to read up on it tonight.'

'Thank you,' said Nancy, acutely embarrassed by his unfriendly reaction and yet not surprised. She—a married woman—had been *flirting* with him, for heaven's sake. What did she *expect* his response to be?

He leaned forward to call in the next patient, but at that moment the telephone on his desk jangled noisily and Callum snatched it up, glad of an excuse to look anywhere than into the soft, wounded brown eyes of his registrar.

'Callum Hughes,' he said abruptly.

There was a pause before a smooth, well-spoken male voice drawled, 'Put me on to Nancy, would you?'

Callum felt the anger begin to rise in him, which afterwards he would justify by telling himself that the man's attitude had been cavalier to the point of rudeness. 'Is it important?' he snapped.

'That depends on your definition of important,' came the cool, unflustered reply, 'but I'd prefer to be put straight through to my wife, if you don't mind, rather than answer twenty questions on why I happen to be ringing her. When I need interrogation practice I'll let you know.'

Callum handed the receiver to Nancy without another word, his face dark, his mouth having thinned to an even more disapproving line.

'Who is it?' hissed Nancy.

'Your husband, I presume,' came Callum's icy reply. 'He didn't actually give his name.'

Nancy's heart sank, wondering why Steve always seemed to take great delight in annoying her superiors. Why, even when she had been doing her hospital rotation he had infuriated the consultant surgeon on more than one occasion by demanding that he take a message to Nancy immediately.

'*When*,' the lofty consultant had demanded of her one day, with barely concealed impatience, 'is that husband of yours going to realise that I have better things to do all day than run around the hospital, calling the junior staff to the telephone?'

'I—I'll tell him,' Nancy had stumbled nervously, as if she hadn't already told him until she'd been blue in the face.

Nancy took the receiver from Callum and put her mouth to it. 'Hello?'

'Nancy?'

'Yes, it's me,' she said quietly.

'Listen. About last night—'

'Not now, Steve,' said Nancy in a low voice. 'Please.'

'I just want to talk to you.'

She could tell from the way he was talking that he was pouting, and she was horribly aware that Callum could hear every word she was saying. 'Steve, I'm in the middle of surgery.'

'You mean you've got a patient with you?'

Nancy sighed. 'Not at the moment, no.'

'So what's your problem, sweetie?'

The problem was that Steve simply didn't understand how important and how *different* her job was to his. However many times she'd tried to hammer it home she'd still failed to persuade him not to ring her in the middle of surgery. She had tried explaining carefully that, as the boss, *he* could so pretty much as he damned well liked, but that she had, first and foremost, a duty to her patients and her superiors which was always eroded by these irresponsible and inconsiderate phone calls.

'I'm busy,' she muttered angrily, watching while Callum pulled a pharmaceutical textbook from the shelf behind his desk and pretended to look up a drug in it.

'How can you be busy if you haven't got a patient in with you?' came his triumphantly flippant reply.

'I'm trying to learn about hypertension!' she retorted, before injecting a soothing note into her voice because she didn't want a row. Not now. Not after last night. 'Look, if you rang me up just for a chat, surely we can talk tonight?'

'No, we can't,' came the sulky reply, 'because I'm going out to a client dinner. I was going to ask you to come with me, but now I don't think I'll bother.'

Thank God, thought Nancy, before guilt rushed hotly

into her cheeks, and she found herself wondering what Callum was making of all this. 'You go without me,' she told Steve woodenly. 'I'll have plenty of studying to get on with.'

'Oh, *fine!*' Steve's response was truculent. 'What a joy it is to be married to a doctor! Well, don't bother waiting up!' And he slammed the phone down.

'Bye,' said Nancy into the mouthpiece, pretending that Steve was still listening as she replaced the receiver, but she knew that Callum had heard and wondered whether she was making the situation worse by pretending that everything was OK. 'I'm terribly sorry about that,' she began, in a low, worried voice.

Callum looked at her pink cheeks, downcast eyes and miserable expression, and had a sudden, almost violent urge to corner her husband to ask him whether he got some kind of kick from upsetting her like this. All his anger evaporated. 'Don't mention it,' he told her gruffly. 'Anything I can do?'

She shook her head.

He threw her a hard, penetrating stare. 'Then let's just get the next patient in, shall we?'

She looked up at him gratefully as he consulted the notes in front of him and called in the next patient. A minute or two later a young woman, who was coughing dramatically into her handkerchief, came in.

Callum made his surgery so interesting and informative that Nancy soon forgot all about Steve and his veiled threats and the rows and the drinking. She forgot everything except what Callum was teaching her.

'You'll discover a definite pattern to general practice,' he told her with a craggy smile at the end of the session. 'Some illnesses are more prevalent in different seasons.'

Nancy nodded. 'You mean more hay fever in summer and influenza in winter?'

'Simplistically speaking, yes.' He found his eyes automatically crinkling at the eager expression on her face, which made her look about sixteen instead of twenty-six. 'But hopefully less influenza in winter these days,' he said. 'We have an extensive inoculation programme operating here, and our flu numbers are down considerably. Preventative medicine at its best!'

Nancy wrote something down in her notebook, then looked up. 'Do you have any comparative figures?'

Callum nodded. 'Some, but I haven't had a chance to analyse them too closely. That might be something you would want to look into while you're here. A local drug company sponsors all the trainees in the area to do small research studies, which are then entered for an award. There's even a cash prize, although. . .'

His voice tailed off as his eyes drifted with reluctant admiration over her outfit. He noted the fine linen of her pale green shirt and the heathery-green blend of her skirt, cleverly cut to make the most of her narrow hips.

'Although what?' Nancy prompted, and her gaze was so clear and so steady that Callum found himself coming straight out with his rather prejudiced thoughts.

'Just that, unlike most of the other trainees, you don't look in particular need of a cash injection.' He shrugged, but the determined pucker of her mouth in response to his remark made him grow extremely uncomfortable.

'That's because I married "well", as I'm sure you've already guessed,' she retorted crisply, and saw him wince, but she didn't care—*he* had started it! 'But maybe if I won it I could buy something for the practice. Or maybe I could donate it to a worthy cause—'

'I'm sorry, Nancy,' interrupted Callum, his green gaze very steady. 'I had no right to say something like that.'

Now it was Nancy's turn to shrug, and she did her best to sound nonchalant. 'It doesn't matter.'

Oh, but it *did* matter. He heard the wobble in her voice. Unwittingly, he had caused her distress, which he'd despised her husband for doing, and that was simply unforgivable. The mutinous look on her pale face told him to drop it, but Callum had never shirked from the necessary, however unpleasant it might be.

'Oh, yes, it does matter,' he contradicted quietly. 'I don't know what prompted it, but I rarely act in such a boorish manner. I hope you'll accept my apology, Nancy.'

For a moment their gazes fused over the desk, and in the silence that followed Nancy felt her heart leap as if someone had jumped out from behind the wall to frighten her.

But as she looked into the mesmeric eyes of her trainer she realised that the feeling she was fighting had nothing whatsoever to do with fear.

And everything to do with desire. . .

CHAPTER FIVE

THE clock on the surgery wall ticked noisily as Nancy attempted to push the unwelcome thought of desire out of her head. But she couldn't blot out the memory. Or the shock of discovering that she found Callum an overwhelmingly attractive man and that, for a moment, he had made her heart leap excitedly in her chest.

But so what? she questioned herself ruthlessly. She was a married woman, and this was what being a married woman was all about. Of *course* she would occasionally feel tempted by other men, apart from her husband—only a self-deluding fool would deny that. Or did she imagine that she would be immune to the charms of other men for the rest of her life?

And, come to think of it, it wasn't really that surprising to discover that other men *could* attract her, not if she stopped to analyse it. Particularly since her own relationship was going through a particularly rocky stage and she was left feeling vulnerable and confused and unloved.

But that was why you married. For better. For worse. You acknowledged the dangers of infatuation and you did your best to put them into perspective.

With an effort, Nancy forced her mind back to the present and smiled as the next patient, a crying and wriggling baby, was carried in by his mother. He was a baby of about three months, and so cross that his cheeks were almost as livid as his distinctively curly red hair!

'Hello, Mrs Markham,' said Callum, with a smile.

Like most parents of poorly children, the mother looked more in need of medical attention than her child! Her face was pinched with worry about her son's health and worry that his perpetual and fretful cry would irritate the doctor.

'Hello, Dr Hughes. I'm terribly sorry about the noise,' she said instantly, 'but nothing I do seems to stop him from being so grizzly.'

Callum gave her a reassuring smile. 'That's what I'm here for,' he told her gently. 'To try and work out what's causing it. You must be the one at your wits end. I only have to listen to it for a ten-minute consultation—you're the one who's subjected to it non-stop!'

'You're telling *me*, Doctor!'

Callum sat the other down and went through the motions of taking a history, but even though he was a very experienced practitioner it was still an effort to keep his mind on the task in hand and not be bothered by the pale and troubled profile of Nancy Greenwood.

He turned his face to her now, and saw that she was all calm and serene attention. Unwittingly, his heart stirred, and his mouth hardened in response. 'Mrs Markham has brought Jack in today because he seems to cry all the time. You will find that this is a pretty common reason for babies being brought to the surgery. I've checked him over and can find nothing abnormal in his chest or his ears. So, any ideas as to the causes?'

This bit was easy—Nancy had most recently spent six months doing a paediatric job at Southbury Hospital, and her consultant had been the most superb teacher.

And, thank heaven, Callum had asked her something she could answer fairly fluently, especially in front of the baby's mother!

'The first things to check for are the obvious ones,' Nancy began, in the manner of a politician about to launch into a lengthy speech.

'And what are they?' Callum interjected.

'The elementary instincts of survival,' recited Nancy rather grandly, refusing to be discouraged and quoting from her paediatric textbook word for word.

Callum frowned. 'Very eloquent,' he told her pithily, 'but we do have a waiting-room full of patients, Dr Greenwood, so can we please have less of the rather florid build-up and a few more facts?'

Nancy flushed, feeling oddly and disproportionately hurt. And how odd that a few terse words from her trainer could inflicted a deeper wound than any amount of bad behaviour from her husband. 'Hunger and thirst,' she answered sulkily.

Callum swallowed. He had felt uncomfortable with her earlier, but this was far worse. Most peculiarly, her pout left him feeling edgy in a very elemental way indeed, and Callum was absolutely appalled with himself for allowing himself to get turned on in the middle of a consultation.

'Would you like to go through a check-list with the patient?' he queried, his cool tone dampening down some of his reluctant ardour.

Nancy, aware that she had been subtly reproached by him, now attempted to put the facts to Jack's mother as simply and as succinctly as possible.

'Many babies cry when they are hungry,' she said.

'But he feeds very well!' answered Mrs Markham

immediately. 'Every four hours on the dot!'

Nancy nodded her sleek, dark head. 'Some babies need to be fed more frequently than four hours, some even more frequently than three hours! Feed times may need to be adjusted, and some babies hold onto their night feeds for longer than others. The same with drinks—if a baby is thirsty it might be an idea to offer him some water twice a day. But I must say,' she added, with a smile to his mother and a tickle on his bare stomach which had Jack visibly melting, 'that it doesn't seem to be a particularly hungry cry to me.'

'I agree with you,' said Callum coolly. 'So, what else can you suggest?'

'Persistent screaming and crying may be the first sign of organic illness or an infection such as otitis media or a urinary tract infection, but your physical examination will have excluded those. As it also included the other possible cause of a crying baby which is, of course, nappy rash.'

'So?'

Nancy hesitated. In paediatrics, they had been taught that emotional causes could also cause persistent crying, but she was also aware that this handy umbrella description could have all kinds of insulting implications for the parents. So she tried to temper her question with as much tact as she could muster.

'Is Jack your only child, Mrs Markham?' she asked.

Mrs Markham nodded and ran a distracted hand through her short, wild hair. 'He is, yes, Doctor. Don't know if I'd have the energy for any more!'

'And do you work outside the home?'

Callum gave a small smile at his registrar's tactful questioning.

'I recently started to work part time as a school dinner-lady.'

'And who looks after Jack while you're at work?' queried Nancy.

'He goes to a child-minder who's brilliant, though she's getting on a bit now and can't do as much as she used to.'

As Mrs Markham explained her circumstances, which included a husband out of work more often than he was in it, an idea slowly formed itself in Nancy's head, and she got a picture of a harassed woman under a lot of stress.

'Do you get a lot of chance to cuddle Jack, particularly as you spend time away from him now?' she asked.

Mrs Markham blinked, as though she hadn't understood the question. '*Cuddle* him?' she repeated.

'Uh-huh.'

Mrs Markham shrugged. 'Well, I cuddle him when I think about it—if I have the time.'

Nancy nodded as the woman's reaction told her most of what she needed to know. 'You have to *make* the time,' she told the woman gently. 'Lack of physical contact can be a cause of persistent crying.'

Particularly in modern society, she might have added, where family units were splintered and couples on the move so much, that a young mother often did not have an older family to demonstrate how babies *should* be brought up. And that good, old-fashioned cuddling cured a lot if ills!

'How come?' asked Mrs Markham, her hand automatically moving to brush the top of Jack's downy head. The baby wriggled in her lap luxuriously.

'Because babies and infants like to be with their

mothers and like the warmth of contact,' elaborated Nancy. 'Firm wrapping in a cot gives contact and sucking a dummy can help. Sleeping in the same room as you might have a quietening effect,' she suggested, but Mrs Markham shook her head with vehemence.

'My old man would leave me if I did that!' she exclaimed, only half-jokingly.

'Well, you might find that if you pick him up a lot— whenever you can—so that he feels happy and secure in the knowledge that his mum is there then he won't cry so much.'

'Just like that?' asked Mrs Markham, raising her eyebrows in disbelief.

'Just like that!' echoed Nancy, recognising the patient's scepticism. 'Honestly! It's worth a try at this stage, in any case. Don't you think?'

'Oh, yes, Doctor, it's worth a try! Anything that might stop him whinging is definitely worth a try!'

Callum glanced up and smiled as Mrs Markham readjusted Jack against her shoulder. 'Let us know how you get on, anyway, won't you?'

'I certainly will, Doctor! And thank *you*, Doctor!' she added, with an extra-wide smile at Nancy.

Callum waited until they had left before he spoke, and when he did his voice was warm with praise.

'That was excellent,' he told her. 'And so sympathetically handled, too! You clearly enjoyed your paediatrics, to have such an instinctive feel for it.'

Nancy glowed like a Hallowe'en pumpkin under his obvious approbation. 'Well, thanks,' she said, then added modestly, 'Although the thanks ought to go to Dr Le Saux.'

'At Southbury?'

'Mmm.' Nancy nodded, remembering the tall, brilliant paediatrician who had taught her so much about babies and children.

'Of course, that's where you did your general practice rotation, wasn't it?' murmured Callum, his curiosity getting the better of him.

'That's right.'

'And why there and not at St Saviour's? Or rather,' he amended, 'since you did your hospital rotation at Southbury, why didn't you do your practice year there as well? Surely it would have been easier because you must have known the area well?'

He regarded her, his green eyes clear and interested. He was obviously waiting for an answer. 'Because—' Nancy bit her lip.

'I'm sorry,' said Callum instantly, as he saw the shuttered look which came over her face and realised that he had been acting most uncharacteristically. Interrogating someone when they were reluctant to answer was normally the last thing he would have done. 'I didn't mean to pry.'

'No, you're not prying,' said Nancy. 'It's a perfectly normal question for a trainer to ask. The reason we moved from Southbury was. . .'

Again her words trailed off because how you could possibly tell your trainer that you had left because rumours were rife about your husband and a beautiful young nurse who was working at Southbury Hospital?

And that she, gutless and placating Nancy, hadn't had the courage to confront her husband with those rumours. Hadn't dared to ask him whether there existed any truth in those claims. She had just been determined to get the two of them as far away as was reasonably possible, terrified that her safe little world was about to explode in her face.

By then she had become known and liked and respected at Southbury Hospital, and reputations didn't come cheaply. And she'd been so close to the completion of her hospital jobs that she'd decided it would be pointless to switch hospitals—but she *could* switch trainers and move away from the area once her hospital rotation had ended.

She concocted a story about the commuting getting to be too much for Steve and wanting to be closer to his parents. All blatant lies, of course, since Southbury and Tenterdon were equidistant to Steve's work and he hardly ever went near his parents.

But she was desperate enough to lie, and it was all too easy to persuade her husband that they needed a break from Southbury. Because by then she suspected that he'd begun to tire of the infatuation.

She heard of Callum Hughes from an unexpected source. She confided in Dr Farrow, her trainer-to-be in Southbury, that she and Steve needed to get away and could he recommend a replacement in an area from which Steve could still commute to his company in Winchester?

Dr Farrow was a wise man, ten years off retirement, who had also heard and been distressed by the rumours which had been circulating. He liked the bright and attractive Dr Greenwood and, personally, he considered that she was wasted on her *louche*, philandering husband. But, as well as firmly believing in the sanctity of marriage, he was wise enough to know when to leave well alone and instead of telling Nancy to dump her husband he simply did his best to accommodate her request.

When she asked him to recommend a replacement trainer one candidate had sprung to mind immediately, and he suggested Callum Hughes.

'I could see if he'll consider taking you on.'

'Won't he consider it an unorthodox request?' Nancy asked worriedly.

Her trained shook his head. 'He needs only to know that you want to transfer, not the reason. Since he has only recently become a trainer he might be keen—and your qualifications are excellent. He might see you as an intellectual challenge.'

'*Me?*' Nancy said, with surprised delight.

'*You.*' Her trainer smiled fondly. 'A friend of mine who taught him at medical school said he was the finest student she had ever come across. And that not only did he have a first-class brain but also a strong streak of practical common sense and a powerful sense of knowing just how to talk to a patient.

'He's a good doctor, Nancy. And he's kind,' he finished gruffly, thinking that Nancy Greenwood looked as though she could do with a little kindness in her life right now.

And that swung it for Nancy. Kindness.

She didn't really care about Dr Hughes's brain or his common sense. Oh, she cared that he was a good doctor, of course she did. She wanted to learn from someone who knew what they were talking about. But even more than that she wanted someone who would be nice to her, that was all, someone to show her kindness. . .

She looked up to find that Callum's green eyes were fixed unwaveringly on her face. Nobody had mentioned his eyes, she found herself thinking mistily as she swam up from the fog of her daydream. Nobody had warned her that eyes could be so green, so intense, so incredibly watchful. . .

Callum watched the extraordinary transformation which began to take place on her face. He found that he could read her like a book. Was she normally quite so transparent? he wondered. He had seen the pain and the bitterness which had clouded her beautiful brown eyes, so much so that he had found himself itching to intrude into her thoughts, demand what was making her feel that way and find out if he, Callum Hughes, could do anything in his power to prevent it.

And then, just as he might have spoken, the pain and bitterness fled, and left in their place was an astonishingly luminescent look of *wonder*. Nancy had gazed up at him, their eyes had met and—quite simply—he had been held in thrall by that gaze.

It had been a moment which had transcended the merely physical, and Callum had been left feeling shaken by the very fact that such an experience had just taken place. To him.

In his *surgery*!

For the second time that morning it was an effort to concentrate on the subject in hand.

'What were we saying?' he asked, as he racked his brains to remember.

'We were discussing the reason I left Southbury,' said Nancy hesitantly.

'But you'd rather we didn't?'

She looked at him gratefully, glad not to have to expose the great, gaping holes in her marriage to this remarkably perceptive man. 'If you don't mind, no. Not just at the moment, anyway.' Because didn't a straying husband indicate a wife who was somehow lacking in the physical allure department?

Nancy felt a shiver of humiliation ice its way up her spine, but was oblivious to the thoughtful look which Callum threw in her direction as he called in the next patient.

Nancy found her first full day in general practice both stimulating and exhausting, and when Callum saw her yawning surreptitiously behind her hand once the final patient had left he smiled broadly.

'Hard work?'

Nancy nodded. 'Very! Although I should be used to hard work after the paediatric job at Southbury—it was frantic!'

'It's always hard work when you start a new job,' observed Callum. 'And general practice is very different to hospital medicine.'

'In what way?' queried Nancy.

His eyes crinkled at the corners. 'You want it in a nutshell?'

'Please!' She giggled, slightly taken aback by the unaccustomed sound of her own laughter.

'I have heard hospital medicine described as working in a zoo,' observed Callum slowly.

Nancy threw him a perplexed look. 'A *zoo*?'

'That's right! All the patients have been neatly classi-fied and labelled according to their illnesses, and each different consultant sees only patients who come under his particular speciality. So if you had a rash you'd see a dermatologist, and if you needed your broken bones set you'd see an orthopaedic surgeon. All highly predict-able,' he finished.

'You make hospital medicine sound really boring,' ventured Nancy.

Callum shrugged. 'I never saw the attraction of it, personally. But general practice—ah, *now* you're talking!'

'Not a zoo, you mean?'

He shook his dark head. 'Not at all! General practice is more like a jungle!' he declared, and there was a quiet kind of passion in his voice which thrilled Nancy. 'No neat labelling for *us*! When that surgery door opens you never know who is going to walk in—or with what problem they're going to present, either. It's exciting! Unpredictable!'

Nancy found his enthusiasm infectious. 'Then the next twelve months should be truly edifying!' she said with a smile.

That smile sent an inexplicable and unexpected whisper down his spine, and Callum sighed softly. After only two days of her company he seemed acutely aware of her as a woman, and he wondered if he was going to be a nervous wreck when the year was up!

'I do hope so,' he said, rather sternly. 'But, in the meantime, I'd better let you go home before you fall asleep, especially as—' he *forced* himself to say it, unprepared for how sour the words would taste in his mouth '—your husband will be keen to hear all about your day.'

Biting back the horribly immature comment about Steve which had sprung to her lips, Nancy instead nodded. 'Oh, yes,' she answered expressionlessly. 'I dare say he can hardly wait to hear.'

Callum heard the bitterness that tinged her reply, and wondered briefly what had caused it. But only very briefly. And he didn't pursue it because it didn't concern him. That's what he told himself over and over again. Whatever the state of the marriage of his beautiful trainee it was simply *none of his business*.

'Off you go, then, Nancy,' he told her, deliberately putting on his most paternal voice, 'and I'll see you in the morning.'

CHAPTER SIX

THOSE early weeks in general practice sped by faster
than any Nancy had previously known, even in her
hospital jobs.

It hadn't taken long for Callum to decide that she was
competent enough to take short surgeries on her own.
He announced this one morning over coffee, and Nancy
almost dropped her cup in sheer fright.

'You can go into the smaller surgery next door,' he
commented blandly. 'Bring some books and pictures in,
if you like.' He then found himself privately and stupidly
hoping that she wouldn't festoon the room with wedding
photos.

'But I don't *know* anything!' she wailed, even though
just yesterday she had commented to one of the receptionists how much she was learning from her trainer.

Callum smiled. 'Rubbish! You know more than you
think. You've also shown me that you have no silly,
false pride, and that you don't consider it a failing to
admit you don't know something. And I'm always here,
Nancy,' he added softly. 'Next door. You only have to
come and ask me.'

Nancy hardly slept the night before her first surgery,
but found the majority of cases surprisingly straightforward.

Only one niggled, and she couldn't quite work out
why. . .

A smartly dressed women in her thirties had

brought her four-year-old son in with a rash.

'This is Charlie, Doctor,' she announced quietly. 'Say hello to the doctor, Charlie.'

Nancy took a full history of the little boy, undressed him, examined the rash—which looked just like a case of mild blotchiness—and even looked it up in her dermatology textbook, which proved reassuring over such vague, unproblematic rashes. Overall, the child seemed well and Nancy certainly didn't want to bother Callum with something minor at this stage.

'Bring him back if the rash changes in any way or doesn't appear to improve, Mrs Berringer,' said Nancy, scribbling away at her pad. 'And, in the meantime, here's a prescription for some cream, which should help soothe Charlie's skin.'

The woman nodded her sleek, blonde head. 'Thank you, Doctor,' she said. 'I will.'

The pace of work was fast and Nancy couldn't remember ever being so frantically busy, especially when a flu epidemic spread through the practice area, fulfilling Callum's darkest prediction. But she couldn't ever remember being quite so interested in her work either, and this was, she was certain, entirely due to Callum.

He was, she soon discovered, not only the most remarkably knowledgeable teacher, but also the most consistent and the most fair.

However busy their workload, he always managed to find the time to explain any medical conditions which she didn't fully understand. He would follow this up with discussing different options for treating the condition—usually asking her which approach *she* favoured before putting forward his own suggestion, which invariably was better!

One of the things he was *very* hot on was follow-up.

'It's no good just treating a patient and then forgetting about them,' he told her. 'We have to see how well the treatment works and decide whether the patient needs back-up support from any other members of the care team.'

So, bearing his words in mind, Nancy called in to see Mrs Anderson on her way back from work one evening. The elderly lady was looking much better since her chest infection had cleared up, her dementia was back down to a manageable level and there had been no more naked wanderings in the garden!

And all because of a few antibiotics,' she told Callum wonderingly. 'Medicine can be like magic sometimes!'

'Sometimes,' he conceded with a smile.

Nancy learned that general practice could be both satisfying and heartbreaking, and that it was good training to try not to get emotionally involved with the patients or their families. This was often easier said than done as she had become very fond of Emma Miles who was extremely sick in a side-ward at St Saviour's just weeks after being diagnosed as having carcinoma of the stomach.

Emma was just thirty-two years old, with the face of a madonna, and Nancy learned that even experienced medical staff could still feel profound shock and disbelief when confronted with such an irrevocably bleak prognosis.

Nancy saw Callum return from one of his almost daily visits to the hospital, his face white and strained and crumpled with the effort of not breaking down. And she found herself briefly longing to put her arms around him and to comfort and warm him, before pushing the thought away as pointless and counter-productive.

As well as trying to learn all the names of the different staff at the health centre, Nancy got to know Callum's two medical partners as well as their busy working schedules would allow. David Davenport was a full-time partner, while Phillippa Gell worked half-time.

At thirty-six, David Davenport was slightly older than Callum, a handsome man whose occasionally stern-looking face disguised the fact that he had a sharp and wicked sense of humour!

Callum told Nancy that David was married to a gla-cial-looking beauty called Cassandra, who had been a very successful model but who had happily given up her career to settle in the country.

'Doesn't she miss the bright lights?' asked Nancy.

Callum shook his head. 'Not at all—and especially not now. She's pregnant, you see. With twins!'

Phillippa Gell was in her late thirties, a small, wiry-looking woman with bright red hair who managed to combine a busy half-time job with looking after three children under ten!

'How on earth does she do it?' Nancy found herself asking Callum one morning before their first patient came in.

'She has help, of course,' he answered slowly. 'But, more importantly, she had energy, too—bags of it, which she puts down to being a vegetarian!'

'Maybe I should try it,' said Nancy thoughtfully.

'Don't you dare!' said Callum, in mock alarm. 'There's little enough of you in any case. And, besides—' his green eyes were questioning '—you aren't short of energy, are you, Nancy?'

'No,' she responded quickly. Just enthusiasm. And she doubted whether a change in diet would alter that!

The one spot on the calendar which stood out in those early weeks was Valentine's Day. Jenny, the practice manager, was sorting out the morning's post, and remarked that Callum seemed to have more than his fair share of envelopes.

'Just how many cards has he *got*?' giggled Nancy, peering over Jenny's shoulder while the stack of envelopes grew and grew.

'Twelve,' answered Jenny with a grin, 'including one which is. . .' and she sniffed at a particularly lurid, pink envelope '. . .liberally doused with cheap scent. *And* another one on which some demure, retiring female has written, "To the Sexiest Doctor in the World".'

'Always presuming it's a woman who sent it,' commented Nancy drily.

She nearly jumped out of her skin when a deep, mocking voice just behind her said, 'Just what *are* you suggesting, Dr Greenwood?'

Nancy whirled round, to find herself staring into a pair of laughing green eyes. 'Jenny and I were both wondering whether extra staff should be drafted in to deal with this deluge of mail for you,' she answered innocently, and then her eyes sparkled with mischief. 'Uh-huh—what *do* we have here?'

A diminutive woman in a dark green uniform, completely dwarfed by an outstanding display of white flowers, staggered across the reception area towards them. 'Dr Hughes?' She smiled. 'Flower arrangement for you. Can you sign here, please?'

Slightly bemused, Callum did as she asked and pulled

out a little envelope which was tucked away behind a spray of roses. The note inside was nothing if not straightforward.

Whatever happened to our dinner date? I know it isn't traditional to sign Valentine notes but, being untraditional and never having sent one before, I'm going to.
    Love, Helen.

Callum tucked the card in his breast pocket, inwardly chiding himself for his reluctance to telephone the luscious blonde actress. What on earth was the matter with him?

He looked down into the clear brown eyes of his trainee and his heart gave an unexpected and unwelcome lurch. *Damn* the woman, he thought savagely, knowing even as he felt it that his rage was misdirected and unreasonable. But what else was he to do, other than feel angry towards her? He simply didn't want to feel this combination of protectiveness and desire for her.

Something was going to have to change. . .

It was soon after that Callum invited Nancy to dinner. 'David and Phillippa and I thought it would be a good idea to meet socially, instead of exchanging a hurried "hello" over the blood forms!'

'Dinner?' Nancy gulped nervously.

'Dinner,' affirmed Callum, with a thin smile.

'You mean, just me—on my own?'

Callum forced himself not to react to her obvious disconcertion—he wasn't allowing her any leeway to refuse the invitation. He tried telling himself that he was

merely interested in seeing what she was like out of
work, and that if he grew to know her a little better as
a person then maybe these ambivalent feelings he had
towards her would disappear, as if by magic.

But the truth behind the invitation was something he
dared not look at too closely. . .

'We rather hoped that you might bring Steve with
you,' he said gruffly.

Nancy's mind buzzed with the effort of thinking just
how she could get out of it. To say that Steve's behaviour
could be erratic would be the understatement of the year.
And these were people she *worked* with, for heaven's
sake. 'He's very busy,' she hedged.

Callum raised his eyebrows, but made no comment.
He'd been on call at the weekend, and had hardly
stopped to catch his breath. He had called Nancy in to
accompany him only on the cases he considered to be
exceptionally interesting—he felt that she needed to
build up a bit of stamina before tackling a full twenty-
four hours on duty!

Nancy caught his expression and read it correctly. 'Of
course, we're *all* busy,' she prevaricated.

'Of course,' he said, keeping his face poker-straight.

'I'll ask if Steve can make the date you suggested,'
Nancy hedged still further.

Some devilish streak made him resist the silent appeal
in her soft brown eyes. 'Well, if he can't then we'll
make another one,' Callum offered equably. 'Since the
whole point of the evening is to get to know the two of
you as a couple, there would be little point in having
the dinner if one of you can't be there. Would there?'

Something in the implacable set of his strong face
stirred an indignant response in her. 'And are *you*

bringing a partner?' she challenged coolly.

'I am,' came the unruffled reply.

Nancy was trapped, and she knew it.

She tried to wait for a good moment to spring the dinner invitation on Steve, but a good moment seemed an awfully long time in coming. In the end, she asked him just before they left for work one Friday since at least she could be assured of his relative good temper and sobriety first thing in the morning.

'*Dinner?*' he scowled, as he poured himself a third cup of black coffee. 'With the *partners*?'

'I'm not suggesting a trip to Siberia,' answered Nancy tartly. 'Dinner is supposed to be fun, you know.'

'What—with a load of stuffy old doctors?'

'Of which I happen to be one—'

'Who don't know how to enjoy themselves.'

'That isn't fair and you know it, Steve,' said Nancy, trying her best to be patient.

'Oh, *isn't* it?' he snarled at her. 'Well, I don't particularly enjoy people watching to see how many units of alcohol I'm consuming!'

'Then maybe you should try cutting back!' Nancy suggested quietly.

Steve went white, except for two livid spots of colour which flared ominously in his cheeks. 'And now *you're* nagging me, Nance,' he said, and his voice held a trace of something approaching sadness as their eyes met.

And Nancy felt sad, too. Unbearably sad. Something between them had changed, something she was loathe to analyse, because. . .

Because if she acknowledged what had changed she would be forced to act on it, and some inner, nebulous fear kept holding her back.

She drew a deep breath. 'Listen, Steve,' she said, and pinned a bright smile to her lips. 'It's a duty dinner, that's all. Something that I simply can't get out of—'

'Don't you want to go, then?' Steve asked her in surprise.

Nancy quickly turned to fill the kettle with water, afraid that Steve might see the guilt in her eyes and the tell-tale pinkness which had warmed the back of her neck. 'No. No, I don't. Not really,' she told him honestly.

'Because—?'

'Because it's a duty thing—I *told* you!' Nancy snapped back, so unexpectedly and so uncharacteristically that Steve was shocked into a compliant silence, which Nancy took to be an agreement to the date she had suggested. She dialled Callum's number with a shaking hand before Steve could change her mind. Or ask her any awkward questions.

Like whether she wasn't a little too old to have a pathetic crush on her trainer after only a few weeks together. . .

Callum chose the venue and opted for Tenterdon's best and most expensive restaurant, causing both his partners to pull expressive faces when he told them.

'Why Tenterdon,' Phillippa had demanded, 'when we could always go to a local restaurant?'

Callum shifted uncomfortably in his chair. Just that morning Nancy had confided in him that she was sick of always being the chauffeur when she went out for the evening because Steve always liked to have a glass of wine. Or four.

And when Callum had asked her why they didn't

share the driving between them she had looked at him as if he were mad, and it had been then that he had decided to choose a restaurant close to their home so that she and Steve could walk there. He wanted to see his trainee relaxed and mellow and warm with wine. All rosy and glowing. . .

'It is *fairly* local,' he observed, meeting Phillippa's gaze.

'It costs an arm and a leg!' Phillippa carried on. 'Why *there*?'

'Because it's the best eatery in the area.' Callum smiled. 'And I am assured that they have an excellent vegetarian menu!'

'With a price tag to match!'

Callum gave a mock frown. 'Phillippa Gell, just how often do you and Julian go out to eat?'

'Hardly ever,' she sighed, with a dramatic shake of her red curls. 'Not with three children and a nanny to run!'

'Exactly!' His mouth curved into a triumphant smile. 'And you are both professional people, are you not? So why not treat yourselves to some decent food for a change?'

'He's absolutely right, Phil,' interjected David Davenport, his eyes twinkling, 'though I suspect that Callum has a hidden agenda in organising this jaunt in the first place!'

'What do you mean by that?' asked Callum sharply.

David looked slightly taken aback, thinking that his partner wasn't usually quite so defensive. 'Why, just that you happen to be bringing a luscious actress whom you clearly want to impress, of course. What did you *think* I meant?'

Callum shook his head quickly. 'Nothing! I'm sorry,

David. I certainly didn't mean to bite your head off! I've been working too much, too long and too hard.'

'I suspect that you're badly in need of distraction in a feminine guise,' observed David shrewdly.

'I know.'

'And Helen Burton is a stunning example of the female variety, though, of course, *I've* only seen her on the adverts!'

'I know,' said Callum again, wondering why on earth he felt that he was simply going through the motions of dating a woman most men would give their eye teeth to be involved with.

He'd phoned Helen the same day he'd received her bouquet, and she had shown just the right mixture of sweet charm and slight embarrassment. He had seen her twice since then—once he had driven to London where they had seen a play by Chekov and then, on a second occasion, they had eaten supper at a quiet country pub close to her home.

Helen lived in Chichester in a sprawling two-roomed attic flat she rented in the house of a fellow actor. She'd invited Callum in after they'd been to the pub, and he had sat drinking excellent coffee while Bach played softly in the background. He'd admired her eclectic collection of art and her slightly outrageous sense of humour, and had wondered why he'd felt not the slightest urge to pounce on her. . .

Nancy walked into the restaurant, and her first impression was that it was opulent yet comfortable. This was luxury on a restrained scale, she thought as she walked through the doors and into the warmth, with Steve trailing reluctantly behind her.

Thank heavens she had dressed up, putting on a fine woollen dress of soft cream cashmere which made the most of her chocolate-brown eyes and the shining curtain of dark hair which tonight she had left swinging free and scented to her shoulders. She wore pearls at her throat and in her ears, and their soft, milky lustre emphasised the fine translucence of her skin.

The others were already seated and drinking but, try as she might, Nancy scarcely noticed Phillippa and Julian, or David and the pregnant Cassandra or even the ravishing blonde who was commanding the attention of the entire restaurant. Instead, her eyes were drawn as if by instinct to the tall, broad-shouldered man with the dark, ruffled hair who rose to his feet as soon as they walked in. Almost, thought Nancy fleetingly, as though he had been waiting for them.

'Wow,' muttered Steve appreciatively, and whistled softly under his breath. 'Will you take a look at that?'

Nancy followed the direction of his gaze with slight confusion. 'What?'

'That' proved to be Callum's date, Helen Burton, and Nancy would have guessed, just from looking at her, that she was an actress—even if she hadn't seen her on a commercial for champagne on television in the run-up to Christmas.

She took a closer look as Callum introduced them.

Helen Burton had all the right attributes, Nancy decided, and in all the right places, too. She had a fragile and slightly old-fashioned hourglass figure and blonde hair that certainly wasn't natural, but when it was that thick and that shiny who cared? Certainly not Steve, thought Nancy with slight distaste as she observed her husband almost slavering as he allowed his gaze to linger on the woman's dynamic curves.

Nancy gave the woman her widest, friendliest smile and shook her hand firmly, but something in the actress's manner towards her alerted her attention. Helen Burton was vaguely wary, thought Nancy with surprise. Surely not wary of *her*?

'Come and sit down,' Callum said with a smile once all the introductions had been made. 'It's boy-girl, boy-girl. Steve, come and sit over here—I've put you next to Helen.'

'I rather hoped you might,' Steve returned smoothly, as he slipped in beside the blonde actress and gave her a practised smile.

'Nancy, come and sit between David and me,' said Callum softly, noting the haunted look Nancy gave her husband as he immediately helped himself to a large glass of white wine. 'Help me choose what to have— I'm hopeless at making my mind up.'

'I can't believe that,' said Nancy, responding instinctively to the warmth in his voice. 'You always seem to be the epitome of decisiveness.'

'Only with patients,' said Callum truthfully, thinking that only his personal life had ever given him cause for doubt. 'And even then there's always room for uncertainty, particularly where diagnosis is concerned.'

Nancy looked up from the menu he had given her to study. 'How come?' she asked, with genuine interest.

'Oh, just that I have a little rule that no matter how glaringly obvious the diagnosis appears to be at the outset to always leave an open mind in case it could be something else.'

'You mean that some illnesses mimic others?' asked Nancy.

Callum nodded as he poured her a glass of wine. 'There is that,' he agreed, 'but no disease should be regarded in isolation. Most illnesses affect many different systems of the body and it is also fundamentally important to consider the psychological ramifications of any disease.'

Nancy sipped her wine thoughtfully. 'Oh?'

Callum steeled himself to resist the velvety enticement of her eyes. 'How a patient reacts, especially mentally, to his or her diagnosis will partly depend on their psychological make-up—'

'And partly depend on?'

He loved the way she interrupted when she was interested. 'And partly on how the doctor handles telling them at the outset. But it's more than just how you give the diagnosis. Your attitude towards diagnostic tests is also vitally important—'

'You mean, don't treat vital tests as a harbinger of doom—'

'But don't trivialise them, either.'

Callum nodded his dark head, and their eyes locked for a distracting moment before Helen's low, musical voice said softly, 'I thought that talking shop was forbidden. Even boring. And, after all, you've always refused to tell me *anything* about your work on our dates, Callum! Haven't you?'

Nancy turned to face the blonde actress, acutely aware of the territorial nature of Helen's words. And who could blame her? She had been gazing, enchanted, into Callum's bewitching green eyes, and what girlfriend *wouldn't* be intensely irritated by such behaviour?

'It's my fault,' Nancy intervened quickly. 'I was the one who started asking questions about work.'

Callum shifted uncomfortably in his seat, touched by her loyalty in defending him and aware that if there *was* any blame to be apportioned then it lay firmly in his direction for *he* had been the one to bring up the subject of patients. And his reason for that had been entirely selfish. . .in that he found himself far less distracted by his trainee when he was forcing himself to think about work.

'Helen's right,' he said heavily, hating himself for saying it and aware of the tiny, crumpling movement of Nancy's soft pink mouth. 'It *is* boring, especially when you have no connection with medicine—'

'Oh, I wouldn't say *that*.' Helen twinkled meaningfully across the table at him. 'I mean, you're *my* connection with medicine, aren't you, Callum?'

Nancy looked down at her menu quickly, aware of the sexual nature of the actress's remark and aware, too, of how painful she found the comment. But she was a married woman, and even if she weren't Callum still wouldn't have dreamed of dating *her* because that would have been a distinct abuse of trust and of the trainer–trainee relationship, wouldn't it? No, Callum Hughes's love life was of no concern to her whatsoever.

'Never marry into the medical profession,' said Steve darkly, staring across the table at his wife as he lifted his glass to his mouth.

Nancy bit her lip. They had argued yet again before coming out this evening. Sometimes she felt as though the atmosphere between her and her husband was so bad that she might crack up. And whilst the intelligent, logical and professional side of her wanted to urge her husband to consider marital counselling, the frightened little girl that lay at the core of her was loath to set the ball in motion.

Cassandra leaned across the table. 'Made your mind up yet, Nancy?' she asked with a smile.

Nancy blinked at her in confusion, her mind still on the subject of marriage guidance, until she realised that Cassandra was asking her what she wanted to eat!

'Unfortunately, I can't manage as much as I'd like to,' smiled Cassandra, patting her pregnant stomach. 'Ever since my pregnancy test came back positive I just don't seem to have the appetite I used to! David says it's purely psychological!'

Dumbly Nancy gazed down at the menu, the print dancing like midges before her eyes.

'I'll have the soup, followed by the sea-bream,' she said.

David Davenport, who was on her left, said, 'Mmm! Sounds good—I think I'll have the same.'

Nancy struggled to find her best, sparkling form, which seemed to have deserted her. 'You're expecting twins, are you, Cassandra?' she asked mechanically.

'Yes! So the scan says! Two for the price of one,' said Cassandra, smiling widely at David. 'Trust my husband to manage to be doubly efficient!'

'You may not thank me for it in six months' time when you're reeling round the house, dizzy with fatigue, with two hungry infants squawling for food in the middle of the night!' put in her husband drily.

'You have a knack of making motherhood sound *so* appealing, darling!' teased Cassie.

'I'm being realistic, that's all!' laughed David.

'Well, if he's being realistic then he clearly intends to help you in every way he can,' said Callum. 'Knowing as he does that new mothers need practical assistance more than anything else if they are to remain sane!'

David pulled an expressive face at his partner. 'Thanks a bunch, pal!'

Nancy managed a weak smile as she tried not to concentrate on the easy, adoring familiarity between Cassandra and David Davenport because it was about as different from the prevailing atmosphere in her own marriage as she could possibly imagine.

'Have some wine, Nancy,' prompted Callum beside her, and she allowed him to pour her some. 'And *relax*,' he urged, so softly that no one else heard.

She tried. She really tried. But how could she relax when all she could see was Steve getting more and more uproarious as the evening progressed? She tried not to watch, hypnotised, as glass after glass of wine disappeared down his throat, but she was miserably aware of how abstemious everyone seemed in comparison to her husband.

True, Cassie was pregnant, and Phillippa and Julian seemed to be heavily into health foods and drank nothing but pure fruit juice. But everyone else seemed contented to sip at a couple of glasses of wine, no more. Nancy wondered what they must think of Steve as, over the dessert, he began telling jokes which would have made a merchant seaman flinch.

'I know a *fantastic* one about a nun and a tablecloth!' he hiccuped.

'Don't, Steve,' Nancy begged him. 'Please.'

'Oh, don't be such a spoilsport, Nancy!' he scoffed. 'Helen's dying to hear it, aren't you, darling?'

Helen's eyes glinted in her direction, and Nancy sensed that she was enjoying herself. 'Sure,' she answered obliquely, 'I always love a good joke!'

Nancy's face was scarlet with embarrassment by the time Steve had finished, and the response to his tasteless joke was decidedly lukewarm. Not wanting to see him make even more of a fool of himself, she sent him several warning looks across the table which he choose to ignore. Instead, he lifted his hand unsteadily in the direction of the waiter and waved it around.

'Can we have some more wine, please?' he slurred loudly. 'In fact, let's have another bottle!'

It was Callum who stepped in and managed to stop the rot, and Nancy could have kissed him. 'Personally, I've had enough wine. Why don't we all have some coffee?'

'Then I'll have a brandy to go with it!' said Steve cheerfully.

Aware that to have refused his request would have created an embarrassing scene, Callum asked everyone else if they would like a liqueur, and Nancy allowed him to persuade her to have a calvados.

'You look as though you need it,' he told her with a tight smile once the chatter around the table had resumed and he was confident that no one was listening to them.

'I could drink the whole bottle the way I feel at the moment,' Nancy offered gloomily.

He shot her a worried glance. 'You can always talk to me about any problems you have, you know, Nancy. I mean that.'

Her gaze collided with that bright green stare and she nodded miserably. 'I know you do.'

'Well, then. . .'

Nancy shook her head. She couldn't confide in Callum, she just couldn't. For surely it would be a betrayal of her marriage vows to pour her heart out to a man she had known for such a short time. A man, moreover, who was not only her superior but also some-one to whom she was becoming inconveniently attracted.

'I can't talk about it, Callum,' she told him in a low voice. 'Certainly not now. Or here.'

'I'm not prying, you know, Nancy,' he answered softly. 'Nor am I experiencing some kind of vicarious pleasure in observing what appears to be a difficult stage in your life—'

'I know that, too!'

He shook his head. 'You can't *know* that, Nancy,' he contradicted gently, 'but I'm glad that you can sense it. I just want you to understand that any time you feel the need to unburden yourself I'm here.'

Nancy sipped at her brandy, and its fiery warmth gave her the courage to smile back at him. 'Whatever made you so wise and so sensitive, Callum Hughes?' she asked him frankly.

He sucked in a breath of pleasure to hear her simple words of praise, then drew himself up short. Careful, Callum, he warned himself. Careful. It wouldn't help matters if he became the all-powerful hero in Nancy Greenwood's eyes. 'It comes with experience,' he told her, far more dismissively than he'd intended, and he saw the shutters come down on her face in response.

'Yes, of course,' she answered dully, and Callum could have kicked himself—hard.

'More coffee?' he asked in an attempt to undo his harshness, but she shook her head.

'No. Thanks. I think it's time we were wending our weary way home.' She glanced up the table to where

Steve was performing one of his party tricks which involved swallowing coffee beans while they were still flaming. Any minute now, she thought in alarm, he would splutter liqueur all over Helen Burton's gorgeous green silk dress.

Hurriedly she rose to her feet. 'We must go, Steve,' she told her husband brightly.

'*Oh.*' He pouted. 'Must we? Can't everyone come back for coffee? Especially *you*, you gorgeous creature!' He smirked in Helen's direction.

'We've just had coffee,' Nancy pointed out.

'And I want some more!' he shot back moodily.

Callum knew one sure way of breaking the evening up, and was disturbed to discover how little the idea appealed to him. . .

'Helen's coming back for coffee to my place, aren't you, Helen?'

The actress met his gaze for a long, deliberate moment, the corners of her wide mouth quirking enticingly. 'You bet,' she murmured, and shot Nancy a sideways glance filled with triumph.

Nancy wondered if Steve was still capable of getting out of the restaurant, without falling flat on his face. Callum possibly sensed her fears for he said, 'Shall we walk your way?'

She supposed it was the only polite way to ask whether her husband needed to be propped up by another man, but Nancy would have carried Steve home herself. Anything other than have Callum witness the humiliating spectacle of Steve really drunk and insulting.

'No, thanks,' she said, still in that bright, determined voice. 'Come on, Steve, the walk and the fresh air will do us good.'

And all she was aware of was the deafening quality of the overwhelming silence that followed them out of the room.

CHAPTER SEVEN

ONE grey morning, when the rain was lashing out of the sky like an angry tongue, Callum arrived at the surgery extra-early in order to tackle the paperwork which seemed to have gone through an alarming growth spurt just lately! He loved the calm of the health centre when it was empty like this although, without the chaos caused by people and their manifold problems, the building took on an oddly surreal atmosphere.

He worked, uninterrupted, for an hour and the only sounds were the rain drumming on the roof, the loud ticking of the surgery clock and the scratching of his pen as he scrawled his notes on the summaries.

It was almost six weeks since the disastrous meal in Tenterdon, an evening which Callum had done his level best to forget but with little luck so far.

He had been appalled at Steve's behaviour in the restaurant, yes. But Callum was no prude—he had been on enough wild rugby tours at med school. He could have forgiven a bout of drunkenness, had he not guessed from his own observations and from chance remarks of Nancy's that such behaviour was habitual rather than an aberration.

The evening had not been a success in other ways, either. Helen had been extremely sulky afterwards and had decided that she *hadn't* wanted coffee but wanted to be driven straight home instead. And when they'd arrived back in Chichester she had very pointedly told him that she was tired, and would he mind awfully if she didn't invite him in?

If he were being perfectly honest with himself, Callum hadn't minded a bit—in fact, quite the contrary. He had felt mightily relieved, though more than a little bit guilty, too. He was well aware of the fact that a woman rarely invited a man into her flat, alone, after midnight specifically for coffee.

Yet in the restaurant he had deliberately implied that he was taking her back to his place for coffee as a way of cutting the evening short to prevent Steve from making an even bigger fool of himself.

Had Helen guessed the hidden agenda behind his invitation? Was that why she had disdainfully refused to take it up? Had she been insulted by his ploy to break up the evening by using her? And, in truth, what beautiful woman wouldn't have been insulted?

For, whilst Helen was everything that most men would truly desire, Callum had most definitely not desired her that evening.

Nor since.

And their complete lack of communication since then bore testament to this.

But in the intervening weeks Callum had put affairs of the heart firmly out of his mind, and had concentrated instead on providing Nancy with the very best vocational training scheme that he could. Whether or not it compensated for the scenes he imagined she was having to endure at home he couldn't tell, but he hoped so.

He found that he was taking her almost daily to visit Emma Miles, who had been in and out of hospital like a yo-yo and was currently undergoing chemotherapy treatment for her cancer.

Callum had been a little wary the first time he had taken Nancy to St Saviour's with him to see Emma— and not just because he had an exceptionally good relationship with his young patient and was worried that introducing another person might have made the dynamics of the relationship uneven. He had also wondered how the two women would cope with the certain knowledge of Emma's death since they were both so close in age.

Part of Callum's skill as a doctor was anticipating problems. Would Emma find herself bitterly resenting Nancy's robust good health? he wondered. And would Nancy find it all too much, having to face the prospect of her *own* mortality?

But there had been none of these added complications. Instead, the three of them seemed to form a bond and a closeness, although this in itself gave Callum a little cause for concern.

'Don't get *too* attached to Emma, will you, Nancy?' he asked her one morning when they were standing together, drinking coffee in the hospital canteen, both visibly shaken by the ravages of their young patient's deterioration.

'I already am,' she told him simply. 'And nothing you can say or do will change that, Callum. But I hope I'm keeping the right amount of professional distance, too. I'm aware that cloying over-involvement would merely be self-indulgent but, oh, Callum, it's so *hard* to detach oneself from the emotional impact of such an early death. Her poor kids.'

'She's going home at the end of the week. The doctor thinks she's fit enough. That's where she wants to be. With them.'

'Oh, thank God,' breathed Nancy, blocking out the bleak corner of her mind which told her that there was little to be thankful for.

As the weeks had moved through into April and a glorious spring Callum had been able to show his trainee the cyclical aspect of general practice.

And that spring heralded the onset of hay fever.

'So early in the year?' she asked him, with her usual wide-eyed interest. They had just bought themselves sandwiches for lunch from the local baker, and Callum had stopped the car by a daffodil-smothered copse to eat them.

'Sometimes,' he answered with a smile, watching the delicate yellow flowers waving their trumpets in the chilly spring breeze. 'In England the illness tends to start dramatically in late May or early June when it's caused by the inhalation of grass pollen.'

Nancy nodded, crammed the last of her avocado and bacon sandwich into her mouth and began to scribble industriously in her note-pad. 'That's the norm, is it?' she queried.

'It is. Though in much rarer cases where tree pollen is indicated it may occur in April or May,' he added. 'And, being in an area with a particularly high preponderance of trees, that includes us!' At that moment his bleeper began to shrill in his pocket, and he quickly dialled the practice on his mobile phone, his frown deepening as he listened.

'We'd better go!' He tossed the last piece of crust out of the window for the birds, and swiftly started the engine. 'Paul Hollingsworth—that fifty-year old carpenter I put on a low-cholesterol diet at the beginning of the month. Remember?'

Nancy nodded. She certainly did! Mr Hollingsworth's normal diet had been a perfect example of what *not* to eat, and had consisted exclusively of stodge and fry-ups. 'Did he stick to the diet?' she asked.

'Pretty much, but he took today off work with vague symptoms of feeling unwell, and is now complaining of chest pain.' He shot her a look as he reversed the car. 'What action might we take if we suspect that he's had a myocardial infarction?'

'Aspirin first,' Nancy answered confidently.

'Why?'

'Because it has an anti-platelet effect—it stops the clot getting bigger if it *is* a heart attack but it must be given in the first twenty-four hours.'

Callum nodded. 'What else?'

'Diamorphine for pain and reduction of anxiety, since any chest pain usually makes patients feel very nervous.'

'Is that all?'

Nancy shook her head. 'No. You also need to give an antiemetic to stop the patient from vomiting and placing extra strain on the heart.'

'Good,' said Callum. 'You certainly know your stuff, Nancy Greenwood.'

'I should do,' came her dry response, 'since you make me read up so much on every subject!'

He smiled again, something he found himself doing a lot of these days. 'Speaking of which, why not look up as much as you can about hay fever and I'll test you on it when you think you're ready?'

'OK,' she agreed, thinking that if Callum had been around when she'd been studying for finals she would have been top of the class!

'I have some books back at the surgery which might help.'

'How many books?' Nancy frowned suspiciously.

'Only two, but they *are* a little on the thick side!' Callum teased as the car powered forward through the country lanes and Nancy laughed and told him that he was nothing more than a slavedriver.

They drove to Mr Hollingsworth's and found him pale and sweaty and blue around the lips. Callum dialled the emergency services while Nancy injected the drugs, and they waited with the patient until the ambulance arrived.

And it gave Nancy a warm glow of satisfaction to know that Mr Hollingsworth's subsequent recovery was in a large part due to the speedy emergency treatment he had received at home.

Callum laid his pen down as the rain continued to patter down on the surgery roof. Only two more summaries, he thought, and then he'd have a clear desk before surgery. And Mr Hollingsworth was coming in for a check-up this morning. He *had* suffered a heart attack, but it had been mild and he was well on the road to recovery, keeping a hawk-like eye on his cholesterol level! Callum glanced at his watch. Where *was* Nancy? he wondered.

Standing outside the surgery door, Nancy pinned a bright and determined smile onto her lips. Only then was she able to breeze in to address the dark, broad-shouldered man who sat at his desk, writing so busily. 'Good morning, Callum!'

Callum looked up as his trainee staggered into the surgery under the weight of an over-full briefcase and an armful of textbooks. He thought that she looked overly fragile in a belted charcoal-coloured raincoat. She was also sopping wet.

His mouth softened. 'Good morning, Nancy.'

He waited until she had deposited the case on the floor, put the books on his desk and hung her overcoat over the peg on the back of the door.

'Those books you lent me—'

'Dry your hair first,' he told her sternly.

'What?' Nancy stared at her face in the mirror and winced as she noted just how thin and pinched and tense her face looked, with her eyes standing out like bright brown beacons. The rain had left her hair dripping in rats tails around her shoulders and the moisture had made it appear even darker than usual so that all the colour appeared to have been drained from her skin, leaving it looking almost transparent.

'You're soaking!' he exclaimed. And she looked exhausted, too, he couldn't help noticing.

His voice sounded almost accusing, Nancy thought, doing her best not to be flattered by what sounded awfully like protectiveness. He would, no doubt, be equally solicitous if one of his receptionists had come in looking like a drowned rat! 'Well, it *is* raining!'

'That fact did not escape me, Dr Greenwood,' he responded drily. 'Didn't you drive in?'

'No,' she said shortly.

Her face drained of expression, and Callum decided to let it rest. For the moment.

'Here.' He handed her a towel, then tried to concentrate on the pile of repeat prescriptions on his desk instead of watching while Nancy rubbed absently at the drying cloud of dark hair which turned into a silken mass that fell to her slender shoulders.

Minutes later she was sitting in front of him with her hands clasped in her lap, as if in prayer. With her pale face and shiny straight hair, she looked about eighteen, he thought, glaring at an illegible note from one of the receptionists as if it had suddenly jumped up at him.

A faint sheen of steam billowed off the still-damp raincoat on the door, and Callum fixed her with a sharp stare. 'So, if you didn't drive in, how did you get to work this morning?'

Nancy sighed. Had he grown up being this persistent, or was it simply a trait he had acquired recently? 'By taxi. The entrance to the surgery car park was blocked with traffic so the driver let me out by the gate—that's why my hair was so wet. It's teeming down out there.'

'And where's *your* car, for heavens sake?' he demanded.

Nancy felt colour creep up round the back of her neck, feeling disloyal to her husband even though he had done nothing of late to deserve her loyalty. What made it even worse was that she knew that Callum disapproved of Steve's behaviour. And the trouble was that she secretly agreed with him. 'Steve borrowed it.'

'Where's *his* car?'

She hadn't planned to tell him—indeed, she hadn't planned to tell anyone—but suddenly the horror of last night's ugly incident came back vividly to haunt her. Her words were bald. 'Steve was involved in an accident late last night. His car was written off.'

'Was anyone hurt?' asked Callum immediately.

It was an exact duplicate of her own appalled reaction when she had opened the door to the policeman at three o'clock this morning. 'No,' she answered tightly. 'No one was hurt. Not even Steve. He was very lucky. He hit a tree head-on and walked off without a scratch. Apparently.'

'What do you mean—*apparently*?' Callum demanded, alarmed at the flatly cynical note in her voice which didn't sound like Nancy at all.

'Just that he didn't come home last night.' She omitted to mention that Steve's nightly absences were becoming unremarkable. 'The police came to the house, looking for him, when they found his car wrapped round a tree.'

'Then where was he?'

'With a friend. Apparently.' There it was, that damning word again. 'He tells me that he was so disorientated after the smash that he walked for miles until he found himself on the doorstep of this particular friend. He didn't want to worry me, or wake me up, so he stayed the night there.'

'But, presumably, the police woke you up, anyway?'

'Yep.' Nancy took a mouthful of cooling coffee. 'And as I didn't know where he was they couldn't find him.'

'And, presumably, since they couldn't find him they were unable to breathalyse him?'

Nancy winced at his perceptiveness. 'Presumably.'

'Very smart of him,' said Callum slowly.

Nancy didn't answer. To agree with her boss would be treacherous, and yet to defend Steve would be hypocritical. She had already spent an exhausting and hysterical morning screaming abuse at her husband when he'd turned up, unshaven and shaking and whitefaced, while she'd been getting dressed for work. She had painted graphic and frightening verbal pictures of how lucky he had been not to have killed someone.

Including himself.

And Steve's response to *that* had been to attempt to take her to bed.

Nancy shuddered now in memory as she had shuddered when he had tried to clumsily touch her, past caring whether her appalled rejection of his mistimed advances would wound him or not.

Callum's voice cut into her uncomfortable thoughts.

'So how come, even though he's been the bad boy, he still gets to use the car while you take the cab?'

'Because it's his car.'

Callum frowned in genuine confusion. 'I thought it was *your* car?'

Nancy bit her lip. 'Steve bought *me* the car but it's in his name. And in times of need, like this morning, he cites ownership as the main criterion for using the thing. I don't even *like* the bloody car! He bought it for me because it suits his image to have his wife drive around in some shiny excuse for a penile substitute! And will you please stop looking at me like that, Callum Hughes, or I'll do something stupid and hormonal— like burst into tears!'

And she did.

Callum flinched.

His instinct was to walk round to the other side of the desk, pull her in his arms and cradle her, but he didn't dare give into it.

For a start, they were in his surgery and if one of the receptionists came in the action could be grossly misconstrued. Because, much as he adored the staff at the health centre, they could be a gossipy lot. And, quite apart from anything else, he suspected that a comforting hug might very well gallop right out of control.

So, instead, he forced himself to react in the same

way he would have done if Nancy had been a patient. He simply nodded, as if she were behaving in the most understandable way possible, calmly handed her a box of tissues and then let her cry. And, by the look of her, a good cry was long overdue.

Nancy couldn't stop sobbing; she couldn't remember ever experiencing such a release of emotion before.

It was as if once the floodgates had been opened she was powerless to stem the flow of bitter, salt tears. She became dimly aware that Callum was speaking to the reception desk, telling them to delay his first patient until he said so and that he didn't want to be disturbed for the next ten minutes.

'I'm s-so s-sorry, Callum!' she wailed, as he replaced the receiver.

'Shh,' was his only response to that.

He carried on writing while waiting for the storm to pass, as if she were doing nothing more unremarkable than reciting what she had eaten for dinner last night.

Not that Nancy could recall having eaten any dinner last night. In fact, meals just lately had been a case of just grabbing whatever happened to be in the fridge— not very much—whenever she remembered. Which had probably added to this stupid weak-as-a-kitten feeling, making her feel like a walking piece of cotton wool.

Only when the sobs had become sniffles, and the sniffles had diminished to the occasionable snuffle die Callum permit himself a small, tight smile. Then he rose to his feet and said, 'I'll leave you for a minute. Wash your face and, if you feel up to it, we'll begin surgery. If you don't then you go straight home and I'll come and see you later.'

Once he had gone Nancy stared blankly at the door.

She was half-tempted to take him at his word and just waltz out of the surgery and go home, where she could climb into bed and pull the duvet over her head and hope that the rest of the world would leave her alone until she felt ready to face it again. Though heaven only knew when that would be.

But home was no longer a haven. If Steve was around there would doubtless be a scene or, worse, a re-enactment of this morning's sordid little tussle when he had attempted to lead her into the bedroom.

And if she went home and Callum was true to *his* word—something she didn't question for a nano-second—and came round to see her then that would surely add even more fuel to the fire. She imagined Callum confronting Steve, or vice versa.

No.

Shakily she rose to her feet, went over to the wash-basin and risked a look in the mirror which hung above it. If she'd thought she'd looked awful when she'd first come into the surgery that was nothing to her deathly appearance now!

She had red-rimmed eyes, clogged mascara and hor-rible blotches all over her cheeks. To add to that was her shiny scarlet nose, which would have guaranteed her a starring role as one of Santa's reindeer helpers, and Nancy knew that she really had to take herself in hand.

She fumbled around in her handbag for her make-up bag and set about repairing the damage so that when Callum returned five minutes later, with another steam-ing mug of coffee, she felt that she *looked* halfway human again even if she didn't feel it.

Callum gave a surprised nod as he deposited the

coffee in front of her. She had clearly slapped on some make-up to cover up the ravages, in the same kind of amount that many women would have considered normal.

Except that on Nancy it wasn't normal. The foundation had evened out her skin tone, and the shadow to her eyelids and renewed mascara had managed to mask some of the puffiness. But she looked like a little girl who had been experimenting with her mother's make-up box, he thought.

Her eyes looked huge and helpless, and her soft pink mouth was puckered into a little rose of bewilderment. He sensed that she was hanging onto her equilibrium by a thread. But the still-damp raincoat remained hanging on the peg and her briefcase was where she had left it.

'Staying?' he queried with succinct surprise, for every other woman he knew would have needed no second bidding to flee from the scene of what could be considered their embarrassing breakdown.

'If you'll have me,' she answered on a gulp.

He drew in a deep breath which was almost painful as he registered how much he wished that he could take her at her word. He felt a deep, poignant urge to kiss away the trembling confusion which still hovered at the edges of her lips, followed sharply by an appalled realisation of why he could never achieve his desire or even speak of it to her.

For she was another man's wife. . .

'Sit as quietly as you like during the consultations,' he instructed gently, 'and join in when you feel like it.'

Nancy sat mutely, making notes, while a succession of patients streamed into the surgery, and she quickly realised that most people were too bound up in their own problems to pay much heed to her.

But towards the end of the surgery she heard a hesitant voice saying, 'Morning, Dr Greenwood.' She looked up into the smiling face of a young woman who was holding a baby.

Nancy recognised the baby first—with those bright red distinctive curls it could be none other than Jack Markham! 'Hello, Mrs Markham! Hello, Jack!' she said with a smile, and offered the baby a rattle which had been lying on the desk. He immediately grabbed it with one chubby hand. 'And how's Jack?' she asked his mother. 'Still crying a lot?'

'Oh, *no*!' Mrs Markham ruffled the curls of her rather solemn-faced infant. 'Jack's fine! The cuddles worked a treat. Even the health visitor commented on the change—said he was obviously much more secure! No, it's me, I'm afraid, Doctor,' she said shyly. 'I think I might be pregnant again!'

Sometimes it was important for a doctor not to react, and Nancy didn't move a muscle of her face as she said, 'I see.'

After Mrs Markham and Jack had left the surgery to pick up a urine sample container from the practice nurse Nancy turned to Callum. 'Do you think she'll be able to cope with such a small gap between babies?'

He finished writing up the notes and sat back. 'Very probably. Most people do.'

'She didn't seem particularly upset by the thought of having another baby,' observed Nancy with interest. 'And she implied that her husband was *pleased* about it, which didn't tie in with some of the rather negative remarks she made about him at the last consultation!'

Callum shrugged his broad shoulders. 'Well, that's procreation for you, Nancy. It makes achievers of us all.' And then he wondered why his words had an unbearably poignant ring to them. As though he could not imagine ever being a parent himself. . .

Nancy saw the sudden tension in his face and wondered if she had stretched his patience too far. He had been so marvellously understanding since she had stumbled into his surgery and started blubbing!

'Thank you, Callum,' she said simply.

He fixed her with a querying expression. 'For?'

'For putting up with my histrionics and not kicking me out—'

But the firm shake of his dark head silenced her. 'I think I am able to judge the difference between genuine distress and histrionics,' he admonished gently, and then put his next thoughts together rather hesitantly— for him.

'And I want you to know that I can be a friend, as well as your trainer, Nancy. I know how doctors can feel isolated when they have problems because they feel that they have to appear to be strong for the rest of the world. But you don't have to be strong, if you feel you can't. Not for me,' he finished gruffly.

Then he called in the next patient so that he wouldn't have to withstand that unbearably attractive look of gratitude which was shining from her big, brown eyes.

Stunned by his kindness and his understanding, Nancy listened in silence while he took a full history from a young woman who was about to embark on her first sexual relationship and who had come to him for advice on contraception.

The girl—Sophie Watkins—was eighteen, and Nancy

knew from her previous gynaecological experience that
a request for contraception at this age wasn't an ethical
problem, as it was if the patient was under sixteen years
of age. She also knew that age was important when the
patient was approaching thirty-five.

'Hello, Sophie,' said Callum kindly. 'What can I do
for you?'

'I think I'd like to go on the Pill, please, Dr Hughes,'
she told him nervously.

He had guessed before she told him, aware that she
had been going out with one of the young farmers for
well over a year. News travelled fast in Purbrook!
Callum smiled to put her at her ease, then wrote in
her notes.

He was used to requests for the Pill, too. As a method
of contraception it was efficient and easy to use, provided that the patient didn't forget to take it! He looked
up. 'Thought it through carefully, have you, Sophie?'

She met his gaze, then nodded. 'Oh, yes, Doctor!'

'Well, we'll certainly consider the Pill,' Callum told
her, 'but there are other methods of contraception which
might suit you better, and which we'll also discuss. It's
best to have as much information as possible. How does
that sound?'

'Sounds good.' Sophie smiled with relief. She had
been terrified to come and see her family doctor. Callum
had known her since she was an eleven-year-old schoolgirl and she had been afraid that he was going to give
her a lecture on sex. Yet here he was, calmly sitting
across the desk from her and treating her like an adult.
Though, come to think of it, she *was* an adult!

'First of all, I'd like to take a general and then
a gynaecological history,' said Callum, 'including

the details of your last menstrual period.'

Sophie frowned. 'I can't actually remember when that was. I guess I could look it up in my diary. Do you need to know exactly, Doctor?'

'I do,' responded Callum gently.

Sophie hunted around in her handbag until she had located her diary, then fixed Callum with a bright, intelligent stare. 'Why?'

'To exclude the possibility of pregnancy,' he told her, and Nancy was struck, not for the first time, by how refreshingly frank he was with his patients.

Sophie screwed up her nose. 'But surely that's why I'm her today—because I *don't* want to get pregnant!'

Callum nodded. 'That's true. But some women don't bother to wait until they are protected before they commence full sexual relations. They might only have had intercourse once, but it suddenly occurs to them that they might become pregnant and so they make an appointment to see me to fix up some sort of contraception, often not realising that they already *are* pregnant.'

Sophie looked absolutely terrified. 'And has that really happened to you, Doctor?'

Callum nodded. 'It really has. Women can and *do* get pregnant after one episode of intercourse, Sophie.'

'Well, not me.' She blushed. 'At least, not yet.'

Callum diplomatically bent his head and scribbled something else in the notes until Sophie had got over her embarrassment.

Nancy listened to the rest of the consultation with interest. Callum was certainly very thorough. Through taking a history, he was able to discover whether Sophie suffered from any conditions which might be aggravated by the oral contraceptive. He also quizzed her about whether she smoked—she didn't—and whether she was taking any drugs which might interact with the Pill.

He then chatted to Sophie about other, non-chemical forms of contraception, but the young woman appeared to have made her mind up what she wanted and screwed up her face dramatically when Callum started mentioning spermicides.

'Yuck!' she exclaimed in horror. 'It all sounds so messy!'

Callum didn't react. It wasn't his job to inform her that there were aspects of sex itself that were messy—she would find that out soon enough for herself. 'It's my duty to inform you of all your options, Sophie.'

Sophie threw him an apologetic look. 'I know, Doctor. Sorry. It's just that I can't imagine using any of the other things you mentioned.'

At one point Callum glanced up and said to Nancy, 'The key to successful prescription of the Pill lies in the assessment of risk factors. Can you tell me what they might be?'

Nancy reeled them off fluently. 'Age, weight, smoking, high blood pressure and diabetes mellitus.'

'Good.' Callum nodded. 'And while one risk factor may be acceptable two or more may not. But. . .' he gave Sophie a wide smile '. . .our patient is of normal weight, she doesn't smoke, her blood pressure is refreshingly low and there is no history of diabetes mellitus. Therefore, she has no risk factors, and so—' He raised his dark eyebrows questioningly at Nancy. 'What kind of Pill do you suggest I prescribe?'

Nancy suspected that he wanted a general, rather than a specific answer as to which brand. 'For a normal young girl who has a normal to light menstrual flow it's advisable to start her on a pill with the lowest dose of oestrogen and progestogen which will control the cycle and have minimum side-effects.'

She looked at him for approval, and he gave a satisfied nod as he pulled his prescription pad towards him and began to write on it in his familiar green-inked scrawl. Then he tore the sheet off the pad and handed it over to a grateful-looking Sophie.

'Here's your prescription, Sophie.'

'Gee, thanks, Dr Hughes!'

He set his mouth in a semi-stern line, aware of how heartbreakingly young she looked. She had assured him that she was in a steady relationship and he had to take her at her word, but he knew that somewhere along the line the odds were that she would get hurt. 'Just take care of yourself, won't you?' His voice was kind but serious. 'And come straight back to see me if there are any side-effects, won't you?'

'I will, Dr Hughes! And thank you!'

Once Sophie had gone Callum turned to Nancy and said, 'Can you list the possible side-effects of the Pill?'

She certainly could! She counted them off against her fingers. 'Breakthrough bleeding,' she began, 'absent menstruation—or amenorrhoea.'

Callum nodded. 'That's right. Go on.'

'Nausea. Headache. Cervical erosions. Depression. Hypertension.' Nancy frowned, determined to remember every single one of them. 'Gall-bladder disease. Candidiasis. Oh, and weight gain! Gosh!' Nancy pulled a face. 'It's enough to put you off the Pill for ever. Not that I—'

She looked up, horrified at what she had been about to say, and flushed a deep scarlet. She had been *about* to say that she had had no use of contraceptive devices, not for ages. But to say such a personal thing to *him*. To her trainer! No, more than that. To *Callum*, she thought with a great lurch of despair she didn't wish to analyse.

Callum both saw and felt her discomfiture and, without being able to pinpoint exactly the cause of it, he could guess that she had been about to tell him something immensely personal. And while the irrational part of his heart sang for joy that she should feel able to speak so freely to him the fiercely puritanical streak inherited from his Scottish mother was appalled at the intimacy which had sprung up between them—a single man and a married woman.

Which he had instigated with his earlier words, by suggesting that he could be her friend as well as her trainer.

'We'd better go and collect our visits,' he told her rather repressively. 'This afternoon is chock-a-block so I've given you your biggest-ever surgery. Is that OK with you?'

'OK,' gulped Nancy obediently. But her misery was compounded by her guilt. What was the point of seeing Callum Hughes as her wonderful knight in shining armour? She was a married woman, albeit in a marriage beset with problems.

But the adult response to *that* was to tackle the problems in her marriage, not simply to run away and fall in love with someone else.

Nancy stared down at her hands in horror, at the plain gold band which was her only piece of jewellery, aware of just how wild and how fanciful her thoughts had become. . .

Fall in *love*?

With *Callum*?

She needed help.

And quickly.

CHAPTER EIGHT

'*MARRIAGE guidance?*' Steve demanded, his voice both aggressive and disbelieving. 'What the hell are you talking about, Nancy?'

Nancy felt a bead of sweat trickle its way slowly down her spine and soak into the fine lace of her bra. She drew a deep breath to try and force herself to remain calm, even though her husband's snarled words came as no great surprise to her. This had been one reaction she had correctly anticipated.

'Marriage guidance,' she repeated quietly, wishing that their house wasn't so unbelievably stuffy. The huge, plate-glass windows certainly had impact and let in an enormous amount of light, yes, but on days like today it was like living in a greenhouse. It was mid-August and they had just returned from a disastrous holiday in the south of France to the hottest summer in fifteen years. And while they'd been away Cassandra Davenport had given birth to bouncingly healthy twin girls!

'*Marriage guidance!*' Steve scoffed, his mouth twisting with scorn.

Nancy kept calm. It had taken her this long to gather up enough courage to broach the subject of getting help for their marriage through counselling, and she certainly wasn't going to blow it now by responding in a similar vein to her husband's inflammatory tone. 'You must

have heard of it, Steve,' she added with a patient smile.
'Everybody has.'

'Oh, I've *heard* about it, all right!' he gritted. 'But
I really don't think we've reached that stage *yet*, do
you, Nancy?'

Nancy waited until she had composed herself enough
to reply. She had already spoken to someone at the
marriage-guidance centre, where a very kindly woman
named Mrs Harford had answered every single one of
her fears. Even though Nancy herself was a doctor, who
had studied and practised a limited amount of counselling in her time, in this she'd felt as raw and as
inexperienced as the next troubled spouse.

'My husband won't be keen to go,' Nancy had confessed.

'Have you discussed it with him?'

'No, not yet. But if we *don't* see someone. . .'

'I do understand,' Mrs Harford had said. 'Believe me,
I do. Well, it could be months before we have a slot
free so you've plenty of time to get him used to the
idea. Why don't you bring the subject up with him?
You might find that just acknowledging that there is a
problem could go a long way towards sorting it out.'

But that had been back in June, and whenever Nancy
had tried to find the right time to mention it to Steve
the right time never seemed to come up. In the end she
had decided to wait until they had been offered a date—
trying the reverse of what she had first intended to do—
so as not to give him the opportunity to talk himself out
of going.

'Well, I *do* happen to think we've reached that stage,
Steve,' said Nancy, then could have kicked herself

because surely that was a very confrontational thing to say. 'What I mean is—'

'Is it my drinking?' he cut across her bullishly. 'Is that what this is all about?'

Nancy spread her palms out in a conciliatory gesture. 'It isn't *just* your drinking, Steve, although you *have* been drinking too much. We both know that. And, obviously, you're drinking too much because you're unhappy—'

'Oh, *please*!' sneered Steve immediately, and defiantly poured himself a vast glass of whisky. 'Spare me all the amateur psychoanalysis!'

'It isn't amateur *anything*!' Nancy snapped back, despite her determination not to rise to any provocation. 'It's professional! And it isn't psycho-anything, either! It's just the two of us, sitting down with someone who has been specially trained to deal with marital difficulties—'

'But you're the bloody *doctor*, Nancy!' he howled. 'If you can't sort out your own problems then I don't know who can!' And he drained the whisky in a single draught and slammed the tumbler down on the coffee-table.

Nancy swallowed, trying hard to quell the betraying yet intense feeling of despair she felt for their future right at that moment. 'Steve,' she began shakily, 'let's not fight again. Please.'

He shot her a devious sideways glance as he picked up his glass and walked over to the drinks cabinet to pour himself another glass of Scotch, ignoring her expression of incredulity when she saw how much of the bottle he had already demolished. 'Why?' He leered at her. 'What else would you rather be doing, Dr Greenwood?'

He saw the way her bottom lip automatically trembled at the suggestive tone in his voice, and his sneer increased. 'No, I thought not!' he taunted. 'God forbid that I should suggest anything as outrageous as *sex* to the high and mighty GP registrar—'

Nancy clapped her hands over her ears. 'Steve! Don't! Stop it!' she beseeched.

He put his glass down and began to move towards her. 'OK, I'll stop it and we'll do something else instead,' he said in an unsteady voice. 'What else did you have in mind, Dr Greenwood?'

She saw from his expression just what he meant and couldn't suppress her first, instinctive response—which was to shudder—and Steve saw it, too.

'What's the matter?' He leered at her again. 'Not interested, Nancy? Getting it from someone else, are you?'

Nancy tried to tell herself that he was responding in a childish manner and that she must keep her head and not fall into the same trap. She was an adult, with adult problems, and she must behave accordingly.

'We have been given an appointment on Wednesday evening at seven,' she informed him slowly. 'I deliberately asked for a night when traditionally you are quiet and when I am never on call—'

'And where is it?' he snapped.

'At the civic centre here in Tenterdon—'

'Oh, for God's *sake*, Nancy!' he bellowed. 'Everyone will know our business!'

Nancy drew a deep breath. 'No, they won't, Steve,' she told him patiently. 'It's completely confidential.'

'Oh, really?' he sneered in disbelief. 'And what happens if someone we know sees us going in?'

'Well, for a start I doubt whether *that* would apply to us,' she told him rather waspishly.

Steve's eyes narrowed. 'And what's that supposed to mean?'

'Just that we know very few people here in Tenterdon—'

'And that's *my* fault, I suppose?'

Nancy shrugged and tried to keep the weariness from her voice. 'I wasn't intending to apportion blame, Steve. I don't particularly care whose *fault* it is—we've both been bound up with our jobs since we moved here from Southbury and we haven't mixed very much. It's a statement of fact, that's all, not a criticism.'

He shot her a suspicious look. 'And what made you so damned assertive all of a sudden?'

Nancy gave him a steady look. 'Why? Does it bother you?'

'Damned right it does! I can't stand aggressive females!'

'Assertion isn't aggression, Steve,' she told him gently. 'It's—'

'It's all to do with that bloody doctor, isn't it?' said Steve suspiciously.

Nancy's heart missed a beat. 'Which doctor?' she asked, in a voice which seemed to come from miles away.

'"Which doctor?"' Steve mimicked nastily. 'Which doctor do you think, Nancy? How about Callum bloody Hughes, for starters?'

'Do you *have* to include a swear word in every sentence you use?'

'It's no good trying to change the subject, Nancy,' said Steve maliciously, revelling in seeing his super-cool wife on the defensive for once. 'I'm not *that* stupid!'

'I've done nothing to be ashamed of,' she defended instantly.

But Steve was a master at manipulation. He knew exactly which buttons to push to tie his wife up in knots.

And intellectually, although Nancy knew what he was trying to do, on an emotional level she seemed powerless to control her instinctive response.

'Not yet you haven't, sweetheart.' And he gave a suggestive smirk which managed to be profoundly insulting.

Nancy's face was bleached of every trace of colour. 'Just what are you implying, Steve?' she whispered hoarsely.

'That you've got the hots for Callum Hughes, perhaps? And that he's got the hots for you, too.'

Nancy trembled. 'Please don't use that disgusting expression.'

He smiled. 'I can word it more accurately if you like, my dear. How about that you'd like Callum Hughes to—'

'Shut up, you foul-mouthed, foul-minded individual!' she flared back.

'Well, I wouldn't hold your breath if I were you, my dear! You may be fairly attractive in a doe-eyed kind of way, but I'm afraid that when compared to that stunning blonde actress there's really no competition!'

'Do you really think I would have gone to the trouble of booking us in for marriage guidance sessions if I was intending to have some illicit liaison with my trainer?' she demanded. 'A liaison which—if it existed in any form outside your sick imagination—would compromise both his professionalism *and* mine! And Callum Hughes is a consummate professional, was well as a fine doctor, so please leave him out of this!'

'Methinks she doth protest too much!' he mocked. 'What's the matter, Nancy—a little too close to the truth, is it? Fancy the sobersides GP with the dazzling green eyes, do you?'

Guilt made her turn on him and confront him with the accusation she had bottled up for months. 'Well, what about you?' she demanded, and it was like lancing a hot, pulsing boil. 'Is this an example of attack being the best form of defence? What about *you*, Steve?'

'Me?' He eyed her warily. 'What *about* me?'

'You and that nurse at Southbury. Oh, yes, of course I *knew*, Steve. You don't have to insult my intelligence by giving me that look of astonishment! Everyone in the hospital was full of it—you would have had to have been deaf and blind not to have heard the rumours.'

'And if they were just rumours?'

She shook her head. 'Don't insult me any more by lying.'

'Wh-what exactly did you hear?'

Nancy saw his face whiten and shook her dark head violently. 'Oh, don't worry, I don't know the full sordid details of what happened, and I have no desire to know, either. I have no idea whether or not you consummated the relationship—'

'Don't you care?' he interrupted suddenly.

Nancy sank down onto the nearest chair as her knees threatened to buckle beneath her. 'I don't know. I just don't know.'

'Nancy—'

'I don't know what I feel any more, Steve,' she admitted to him honestly. 'Like I can't understand how or why I have pretended for so long that nothing was wrong. Why I buried my head in the sand as though nothing was happening.'

'The girl meant—'

'No!' Her voice was so unaccustomedly icy that Steve recoiled in surprise. 'No clichés, I beg you. Whatever happened between you she must have meant something. Intimacy can be much more than just sex, you know, Steve. Intimacy can be having a level of communication and understanding with someone who isn't your spouse. And that degree of intimacy can be just as damaging and as hurtful as a brief night of sex with someone else.'

She felt a dull, pink colour rise in her cheeks and wondered what right she had to lecture Steve for wasn't she precariously close to a similar stage of understanding with the man who was her boss?

Steve put his empty glass down on the table, and eyed her thoughtfully. 'So, what do you want to do next?'

Nancy regarded him steadily from her chair. The quality of unreality which had been pervading her life for the past weeks was now overwhelmingly strong. Just who *was* this man to whom she was legally bound?

Once she had been enchanted by his sparkling blue eyes and boyish charm and lantern jaw, but all the light had gone from his eyes now and his once-healthy complexion was tainted with the ruddy flush of excess alcohol. Had *she* done that to him?

But Nancy drew herself up short, finding herself imagining what Callum would say if she posed the same question to him.

He would tell her that ultimately no one is responsible

for someone else's behaviour—that individuals do and must bear culpability for their own actions. *She* hadn't driven Steve to drink. He was drinking too much, yes, but whether that was because he was using alcohol to escape the problems within their marriage or whether he simply had a growing problem with substance abuse, Nancy couldn't tell.

But was she really any better than Steve? If he had blotted out the pain and the reality of their marriage with booze had she not been guilty of a similar type of escapism? She had buried her head in the sand over his infatuation in Southbury. She had allowed the affair to change the course of their lives, without once ever challenging him over it. Was she really so weak and so afraid that she couldn't face the truth, however unpalatable?

'I thought that counselling might help us get our problems sorted out,' she told him.

'But not any more?'

Nancy hesitated as she met the question in his blue eyes, remembering what her parents had drummed into her about stability and structure—about the importance of seeing through what you had begun. About commitment, too.

But marriage. . .

Was it enough to believe so strongly in marriage that you were prepared to paper over the cracks? For wouldn't that just leave her with a rotting framework of a life?

There were no children involved. Would it not be better if they both admitted that they had made a dreadful mistake? To cut their losses and leave now—before they inflicted even more pain on each other?

Nancy stared down at the shining gold wedding band on her finger, which at that moment seemed to symbolise all that was unsatisfactory in her life.

She remembered when Steve had placed the ring there, on a bright autumn day at Camden registry office, with a group of their friends giggling in the background. Most of those friends had scattered now, dispersed by jobs and conflicting lifestyles. And, if Nancy was being particularly honest, most of *her* friends had disappeared from the scene because they hadn't liked Steve.

But she, Nancy, *had* liked him. More than that, she'd loved him enough to marry him. If she gave up on their marriage now wouldn't that leave her wondering for the rest of her life if she was unable to commit to and sustain a relationship?

'Nancy?'

She realised that Steve was waiting for an answer. And even before she opened her mouth Nancy realised that some things never changed, and that she was about to behave as she had always behaved—as she had been brought up to behave. To do what she believed to be the *right* thing. To listen to her head, rather than follow her heart.

'I think we should go for counselling,' she told him, but couldn't fail to see the unmistakable look of disappointment which momentarily crossed her husband's coarsened features. And Nancy shuddered, aware of the irrevocable step they were about to take. . .

For the rest of that evening and all of the next day Nancy was unusually distracted, which didn't excuse what happened during her afternoon surgery but at least partly explained it.

It was the busiest section she had experienced as a

trainee, and it took every ounce of concentration she had to keep from running over time. The temptation was to spend far more time than the allotted ten minutes, just talking to the patient, but Nancy knew that it simply wasn't practical to do so.

She dealt with the usual summer mixture of hay fever, allergies and bugs picked up from holidays abroad. She phoned a patient to tell him that the biopsy of a lump in his neck was benign, and then rang the social worker to see if there was any chance of Dolly Anderson getting out of her house for the day.

'Maybe to the seaside?' Nancy suggested. 'As the weather's so hot.'

'I'll see what I can do,' promised the social worker, then added jokingly, 'There's a nude beach at Brighton, isn't there? Perhaps Dolly would like to go there?'

'She'd be absolutely *horrified*!' said Nancy truthfully, as she put the phone down.

She pressed the intercom for her next patient. 'Charlie Berringer to see Dr Greenwood, please.'

Nancy creased her forehead in a slight frown. Young Charlie Berringer and his mother were among the most frequent visitors to her surgery. The little boy's blotchy rash had cleared up spontaneously, but the following week his mother had brought him in with a headache, although overall Nancy could find nothing wrong with him.

Then a couple of weeks ago they had returned to the surgery because Charlie had diarrhoea and vomiting, but Nancy had thought that the child looked well and had advised nothing more than a twenty-four-hour stomach rest, taking, clear, sweet fluids only.

Mrs Berringer opened the door and pushed Charlie

into the surgery, and once again Nancy was struck by how beautifully co-ordinated the woman's clothes were. Mind you, she always wore pastel shades, which set off her ash-blonde hair to perfection, but Nancy wondered how on earth she could keep them so exquisitely *clean*— particularly with a four-year-old boy around!

'Sit down, Mrs Berringer,' said Nancy, with a smile. 'How's Charlie's diarrhoea and vomiting?'

'Oh, it cleared up after he had the clear fluids for twenty-four hours, like you said,' replied Mrs Berringer vaguely. She sat down and clasped her hands together in her lap, then looked at Nancy.

'So, what seems to be the problem today?' prompted Nancy politely.

'Oh, it's Charlie again, Doctor. He seems to have a very sore bottom.'

Nancy nodded and wrote in the notes. 'This can often be the case after a bout of diarrhoea,' she told the woman with a kind smile, designed to put her at her ease. 'I'd better take a look.'

She cajoled Charlie onto the examination couch and examined him, and when she had finished washing her hands she sat back down opposite his mother. 'It *is* a little sore,' she agreed, though thinking that, to *her* mind, it didn't seem sufficiently severe to merit a doctor's appointment. But, there again, that was an easy distinction to make when you were medically qualified.

'I'm going to give a prescription for some cream, which will ease the irritation around Charlie's bottom, Mrs Berringer,' she said, and decided that a little gentle confrontation might be in her patient's best interests. 'Perhaps you'd like me to give him a complete check-up, as you've seemed rather concerned about him just lately?'

'You mean *now*?' asked Mrs Berringer, her ash-blonde hair swinging in a perfect, glossy bell.

Nancy glanced at her watch. She wanted to talk this through with her trainer, but Callum was visiting Emma at St Saviour's and probably wouldn't be back yet. Meanwhile *she* still had her last patient to see.

'Not now, no. But we could book you in for an appointment at the end of the week. As it's non-urgent,' she added reassuringly.

'Sure,' agreed Mrs Berringer, nodding obediently. 'Come on, Charlie, time to go—and put that book *down*!'

Nancy's last patient was a twenty-three-year-old temporary resident, which meant that he wasn't registered with the Purbrook practice or, indeed, with any practice in the area. He had matted hair to his shoulders and his chalk-white face was pinched with pain, which made him look much older than he really was.

Nancy glanced up, her heart contracting automatically as she saw how ill he looked. 'Mr Alan Worthington?' she said.

'That's right, Doc!' he groaned, clutching at his abdomen.

'Sit down, Mr Worthington, won't you? Tell me what seems to be the problem.'

The problem came pouring out in a harrowing account. Mr Worthington had terminal carcinoma of the stomach. He had been given under six months to live and, looking at him, Nancy thought he would be lucky to last that long.

'I'm staying with a friend here in Purbrook, but I've

run out of painkillers, Doc.' He winced. 'If I don't have something soon I don't know what I'll do. I'm climbing the walls with the pain!'

Nancy didn't doubt his distress for a moment—it was abundantly clear from the clammy pallor of his skin. But she had no idea how to handle a case such as this. 'Can I have the name of your GP, Mr Worthington?' she asked.

'Sure. It's Foreman,' he said swiftly. 'Dr Dick Foreman—he's in Salisbury.'

Nancy nodded. The name of the well-known medical intellectual was familiar to her. 'Would you excuse me for just a moment?'

He nodded his shaggy head.

Nancy went and tapped on Callum's door, mightily relieved to find him in—and alone. She recited all the facts to him.

'Better check with his GP,' said Callum at once, 'just in case he *is* an addict. To cover yourself.'

'That's what I thought,' said Nancy, and went back to her surgery to discover that not only had her patient disappeared but so had a whole prescription pad.

The police were called, and after Nancy had given them a full statement she went straight along to see Callum, who had already spoken to them.

'Oh, I feel such a *fool*!' she exclaimed.

'It was a mistake, Nancy,' he commented mildly. 'Everyone makes them.'

'So *naïve* of me!' she complained. 'Especially as he even *looked* like a drug addict!'

He smiled. 'Don't be so hard on yourself! At least you aren't guilty of making value judgements. What did the police say?'

'That we have to use green ink only on our prescriptions for the next three months so that if Mr "Worthington" tries to use any of the scripts locally the pharmacists will be aware that they are forgeries. Oh, and I've rung Dr Foreman in Salisbury to tell him that his name is being bandied around by an unscrupulous addict. He was very philosophical about it.'

'Good. Now why don't you sit down?' urged Callum gently, observing how drawn her face had been of late. 'And tell me—is there anything else worrying you?'

'Yes, I'm afraid there is,' she responded.

'What?' Callum found himself leaning forward eagerly, ridiculously disappointed when she started telling him all about Charlie Berringer and his minor ailments.

'It's perplexing,' she mused, 'because his mother keeps bringing him in and there's nothing much wrong with him. I've offered to check him over to put her mind at rest.'

'Perhaps you're treating the wrong person,' suggested Callum thoughtfully. 'How is *Mum*?'

'She's fine!' said Nancy instantly. 'Very glam and beautifully made-up—'

'Depressed?' he hazarded.

'Callum!' Nancy exclaimed indignantly. 'She's full of beans and so well organised that she puts *me* to shame!'

'Nancy!' mocked Callum softly. 'Have you never heard of smiling depressives? Who can't quite bring themselves to admit to a problem so they keep concocting flimsy excuses to bring them to the surgery in the hope that the doctor will pick up on their non-verbal clues.'

He was right, of course. As usual.

When Nancy called Mrs Berringer in for her appointment, after suggesting that she leave Charlie at home, it all came tumbling out in a torrent of tears.

How she was terrified of the disruption and untidiness that a small child could wreak on an immaculate house. How she was worried that her husband was having an affair.

Initially, after further discussion with Callum, Nancy prescribed anti-depressants for Mrs Berringer and, after offering to see her and her husband together so that she could mediate if there *were* marital problems, she enlisted the help of the health visitor to support the family.

It was the type of case which made Nancy realise simultaneously how much she enjoyed the work and yet how much she still had to learn.

'I should have picked it up myself, really!' she told Callum later that month, after seeing a hugely improved Mrs Berringer whose fears about her husband's infidelity had proved unfounded.

'Well,' he said with a shrug, 'you guessed that *something* was up, didn't you?'

'Yes,' she murmured reflectively. 'I suppose I did.' She looked into his eyes. 'Thanks, Callum,' she said very softly.

'My pleasure,' he replied, hoping that his voice didn't sound in any way wistful.

CHAPTER NINE

'I'M GOING to see Emma,' said Callum, putting down the phone with a heavy hand, while outside the relentless November winds buffeted the trees against the boundary fence.

Something unbearably sombre in his tone made Nancy look up from the notes she was making, following one of Callum's brief talks on jaundice. After a good deal of thought, she had decided not to sit her membership exam the previous month. She was too committed to her marriage guidance sessions and too caught up and fraught with wondering what was going to happen to be able to study in earnest. She had decided to sit the exam in May, though she had been deliberately vague when Callum had asked her the reason.

'How is she?' she asked in a soft voice, dreading the cruel inevitability of his answer.

He met the question in her eyes painfully. 'Emma's dying. She took a turn for the worst just after breakfast this morning. It seems. . .' He hesitated, his gaze drawn helplessly to the ceiling where a blue metallic balloon, bearing the message, CONGRATULATIONS! was incongruously floating. How it had found its way into his surgery he didn't know. 'Oh, *hell*!' he exclaimed bitterly.

Nancy followed the direction of his gaze, understanding the misery on his face perfectly. Jane Slade, the youngest of the receptionists, had gone into

133

labour yesterday and had produced a huge baby boy. A triumphant entry into life just as one of the practice's much-loved patients was about to undergo a tragically premature death.

Nancy swallowed. 'It *is* hell but that, I'm afraid, Callum, is life,' she whispered softly, wondering why it was that the fundamental truths always came out sounding like trite clichés.

'And death,' came his bleak response, his voice unsteady, his green eyes looking suspiciously bright.

It was the first time in all the months of working for him—even through Emma's illness—that Nancy had ever seen him quite so distressed, and she blinked with surprise and disquiet, then glanced down at her watch.

Steve had warned her that he was going to be late tonight. It was one of the strategies suggested by their marriage-guidance counsellor. Such dialogue was supposed to open up channels of communication. No longer would Nancy have the indignity of now knowing where her husband was, and no longer would Steve have the guilt of not being totally honest with his wife.

Except that Nancy suspected he *was* being elusive with the truth. And she knew that before she fell once again into the trap of simply ignoring what she preferred not to contemplate she was going to have to say something to him. . .

'Can I come with you?' she asked Callum tentatively. 'To see Emma? Unless, of course, you'd prefer to go on your own?'

His green eyes darkened. 'Would you, Nancy?' he questioned simply. 'I'd like that. For Emma. And for me,' he added.

'For you?' she asked, somewhat startled.

He acknowledged her surprise with a wry nod of his dark head. Was that how she saw him? he wondered. Calm, capable Callum with a heart that was never stirred by tragedy? 'Don't you think I get affected too, Nancy?' he asked. 'Is that because I'm a man or because I'm a doctor?'

'I didn't mean to—'

He shook his head to silence her, as if the words were heavy burdens he needed to shed. 'I've known Emma since I first came to this practice,' he told her quietly. 'She's almost exactly the same age as me, and we hit it off straight away. She told me about the best part of living in this part of the world—and the worst parts, too! She used to make cakes for Christmas and my birthday, and I. . .delivered her last baby.'

His voice shook very slightly before he felt able to continue. 'When she first came to me with vague symptoms I didn't want to listen—'

'You? Not listen?'

In spite of everything, his spirits were lifted fractionally by her obvious faith in him. 'I wanted it to be anything—*anything* but the one thing I knew in my heart it really was. I ordered every investigation under the sun, and then had her rushed into St Saviour's. Which happened to coincide with my holiday. Skiing.'

'That was just before I arrived, wasn't it?'

He nodded, and looked at her properly then. 'Yes, it was.' Dear Nancy, he thought with genuine affection. She still looked small and fragile, he thought—the 'wee thing' of his initial impression. But her hair had been cut a couple of months ago and the dark glossy strands now fell in a bell to her shoulders, which suited her far more than the severe, scraped-back style she'd previously adopted. Her clothes had become less austere and restrained of late, too. He wondered what had brought about these changes.

Callum sighed. Was it really getting on for a year since Nancy Greenwood had first entered his life? What on earth was it going to be like when she found herself another practice and moved on?

He was going to miss her.

Quite badly.

Nancy suspected that Callum had very few people to whom he could unburden himself. He wasn't married, and Helen Burton—if, indeed, Callum was still seeing her—didn't strike her as the kind of woman who would be prepared to listen to the less palatable details of illness. In fact, from a couple of remarks the gorgeous actress had made in the restaurant that night she had come over as very squeamish indeed. And, as Callum himself had once said, doctors could be the most isolated people in the world.

Sometimes, like now, it was important and cathartic that he should be able to express his natural feelings of sorrow and frustration and guilt. 'And you felt bad about being away when Emma was diagnosed?' she guessed.

He gazed at her sombrely, grateful for her perception and for her gentle way of showing it. 'I felt terrible,' he confessed. 'So bad that I almost cancelled my holiday—'

'Then why didn't you?'

He almost smiled. Anyone else might have scoffed at him for even contemplating such an extravagant gesture towards a patient. But not Nancy. Sweet, understanding Nancy.

'Because I knew that Emma wouldn't want me to.

And because I was certain that she had already guessed that her prognosis wasn't good. Emma wanted to be strong for her family, and if people around her started crumbling then it would be letting *her* down in a way.'

Nancy nodded thoughtfully, understanding perfectly. She put her pen away and stood up.

'Come on, then, let's go,' was all she said. Noting the lines of strain etched around his craggy features, she added on impulse, 'Shall I drive?'

He flashed her a grateful smile. 'Would you mind?'

'Only if you promise not to spend the whole journey making barbed comments about women drivers!'

'Nancy!' He struck his chest in a gesture of being woefully misunderstood. 'How could you accuse me of behaving in such a sexist manner?'

'So you won't?'

'That depends,' he teased, 'on what I think of your driving!'

They walked out through the reception area where they were waylaid by Jenny McDavid, who was holding an enormous bouquet of pale blue and white flowers tied with an extravagant blue bow.

'I know you said you were going to visit Jane and the baby in hospital,' she said, sniffing at the blooms with pleasure. 'These arrived just after some of the girls went up to see her and I wondered if you could take them.'

Callum shot Nancy a questioning look. It would inevitably be an assault on the emotions to visit a brand-new baby just after bidding farewell to Emma. And, of course, he *could* face it on his own but, frankly, he would rather have Nancy with him.

She nodded at his wordless question. 'I'll come,

too, if you think Jane wouldn't mind.'

He smiled. 'Why on earth would she mind?'

They walked out to the car park, and Callum found himself searching fruitlessly for Nancy's scarlet little sports car. He was slightly taken aback when she pointed towards a glossy black Swedish saloon which, although powerful, was infinitely more subtle than the machine he had been expecting.

'I'm over there,' she said.

He raised his brows. 'Whatever happened to the "penile substitute"?' His mouth twitched with amusement at the corners as he quoted her heated words.

Nancy blushed like a schoolgirl. 'Oh, don't! I shouldn't have said that!'

He found the blush quite enchanting. 'But why not?' he shrugged. 'It was a fairly accurate description.'

'I decided that I wanted a change,' she told him as they climbed in and she started up the engine.

'I see.' He was curious, but he said nothing more. It seemed inappropriate somehow to be quizzing Nancy about her car and what had brought about such a change when he knew the difficult task which lay ahead of him. Instead, he simply buckled up his seat belt, leant back in the seat and observed her driving technique.

Nancy knew that he was watching her and it should have made her nervous but, oddly enough, it didn't. She hated driving Steve. He fiddled around with all the knobs and switches, constantly moaned that she was driving too close to the kerb or to other cars, or that she was driving too slowly, or not indicating quickly enough or indicating when she shouldn't be. However Nancy drove it was never good enough for Steve.

'Do you want some music?' she asked.

'I don't think so, do you?'

'No.'

They drove in silence and it was the easiest silence Nancy had ever experienced—which again was odd, considering that both their thoughts were immensely sad. But by the time that Nancy drew up in front of Emma's house they had composed themselves, outwardly at least.

The house had the unnatural hush of impending tragedy.

Emma's mother answered the door, her face lined with strain and grief. Two of Emma's children clung in bewilderment to their grandmother's skirts. The elder of the two was a boy of around ten. His eyes full of anger at an event beyond his understanding. Meanwhile, his sister—younger by two years—sucked her thumb and made low, grizzling sounds like a wounded animal. From a distance, in one of the downstairs rooms, could be heard the robust yell of a crying baby.

'Hello, Dr Hughes,' said the grandmother. 'It was good of you to come. Please, come in.'

'This is my trainee, Nancy Greenwood,' said Callum, as he stood back to let Nancy precede him.

Emma's mother nodded her head. 'Yes, we met once before at St Saviour's. And Emma has mentioned you.'

Callum ruffled the boy's hair. 'Do you want to take me up to see Mummy?'

The boy nodded, grave and pale, and took them both up to the sick room.

On the bed—a tiny shrunken figure now—lay Emma, her once beautiful face hollowed out by the damage the disease had inflicted on her body.

When Nancy had visited Emma in hospital she had

been surrounded by the paraphernalia of medicine, hooked up to drips and tubes and bags and bleeping machines. But now medicine had admitted defeat, and her frail arms were unencumbered by equipment.

Her husband sat as close to her as possible and gripped Emma's bony hand, the effort of keeping his emotions in check making his face appear a tight, tortured mask.

Emma had been dozing, but at the sound of footsteps her eyelids fluttered open. She smiled longingly at her little boy and then her gaze transferred to Callum, with Nancy behind him, and she held out her hand in an almost imperious beckoning movement.

'Callum,' she said hoarsely. 'Nancy.' Then she said softly to her husband, 'Take William down, will you, John, darling? Give me five minutes. William, come and give Mummy a kiss.'

The little boy lent gingerly over the bed and planted a kiss on his mother's jaundiced cheek, and it was as much as Nancy could do not to burst into bitter, disbelieving tears. But she thought back to what Callum had said earlier.

It wouldn't be fair to Emma. She needed their strength right now, not their weakness. She needed to know that they would all pull together after her death for the sake of her husband and her mother and—most importantly—for her children.

'Sit down,' she whispered, a small smile lifting each corner of her dry lips as they perched on opposite sides of the bed. 'Don't let the nurse see you!'

Callum picked up her hand and covered it in a strong, warm clasp. 'You look—'

But Emma shook her head. 'No, Callum, don't,' she pleaded. 'There isn't time. . .'

Their eyes met for a long, painful moment. 'No,' he answered, with difficulty.

'I just want you to promise me one thing.' She frowned. 'Two things,' she amended, and cleared her throat.

'Anything.'

The faintest trace of humour flashed in eyes made huge by a wasted face, and Nancy found herself fervently wishing that she had known Emma when she was well. 'You may have just compromised yourself!' she croaked.

'Tell me,' said Callum softly, and bent his ear to the sick woman's mouth.

'The children—'

He knew what she wanted to say, without her speaking another word. Indeed, he had known on the way over which thought reigned supreme in her mind. 'We'll look out for them. All of us. The practice, the village, everyone. And we'll offer John help—practical help. You mustn't worry about them, Emma. I give you my word.'

Emma slumped back against the pile of pillows and closed her eyes. 'Thank you.'

They sat in silence, listening to the sound of her laboured breathing, and Nancy thought that she must have fallen asleep but her eyelids fluttered open once more and she fixed her gaze first on Callum and then on her.

'Second thing,' she managed, and Nancy leaned over to dab gently at her dry lips with some moistened cotton wool.

Callum steeled himself for something equally distressing, praying that Emma's remarkable courage and fortitude didn't mean that she was about to mention her own funeral.

He honestly didn't think he could take it.

'What?' he whispered.

'You should. . .marry.' Emma drew a deep breath, and then her head turned to face Nancy. '*Her!*'

There was a stunned silence. Nancy couldn't bear to look at Callum, but she did look at Emma. And could have sworn that she saw the faintest whisper of a wink. Had she forgotten that Nancy was already married?

'Now give me a kiss goodbye,' croaked Emma, 'and send John and the children up.'

Nancy left the house in a daze, stumbling on the path as the front door closed behind them. Callum's hand shot out automatically to steady her. His brief touch was the best thing that had happened to her in a long while, but he snatched his hand away as if scorched and Nancy dragged in a deep breath in an attempt to pull herself together.

Neither of them said a word as they strapped themselves into the car, and only when Nancy started the engine was the silence broken.

'To the hospital?' she asked, but he shook his head.

'I couldn't,' he said through gritted teeth. 'And if you think that sounds selfish then you're damned right!' He leaned back against the headrest. 'But it isn't just selfish. It isn't fair to Jane, either. Or to her husband. There is no way I could conjure up any emotion right now other than howling rage. And that's the last thing that either of them need. This is one of the most joyful days of their lives—it wouldn't be fair to inflict our grief on them.'

Nancy glanced over her shoulder to where the extravagantly tied bouquet of blue and white flowers was looking in dire need of water. 'What about the flowers?' As soon as she asked the question she was aware of how inconsequential it was.

'I'll order more tomorrow.'

'How about a drink, then?' she suggested tentatively, loath to leave him looking so wretched. 'But I don't suppose you can face going into the pub, either?'

'Not really. Can you?'

'No.' She revved up the engine. 'I'll take you home.'

'My car is still at the health centre—'

'You can collect it tomorrow,' she told him crisply. 'You're in no fit state to drive.'

'And are you?'

'I think so.'

'Thanks, Nancy.' At that moment he valued her strength even more than her lack of concern at the role reversal which seemed to have taken place. He couldn't think of another woman he would be comfortable with, seeing him so knocked for six like this.

This time there was also silence in the car, but it had lost all its easiness. Whether it was because they had just, in effect, bade farewell to a brave and lovely woman, or whether it was because of the dramatic thing she had said to them, Nancy didn't know. All she did know was that she felt like there was a great, gaping hole in her heart, and she wondered how on earth she would ever be able to fill it.

After months of accompanying her trainer around the district, Nancy now knew the practice area like the back of her hand. Callum had once pointed out where he lived when they had been out on visits together but this was the first time she had ever driven up close to the thatched cottage.

As the car slid to a halt Callum was terribly tempted to invite her inside. Maybe they *needed* to talk—to clear the air a little after Emma's bombshell. But the last thing he wanted was for his action to be misconstrued in the light of what had been said.

'Would you like to come in for a drink?' he asked. 'Or a coffee? Or do you have to rush home?'

'No,' she answered slowly. 'No, I don't.'

He let them into the cottage, where he had to dip his head to get through the low, beamed doorway, and snapped on a light switch so that three small lamps immediately gave out a soft, peachy glow.

Nancy gave an instinctive little gasp of pleasure as she stepped straight into the sitting room, her first impression being of books and brasses and clutter. It looked so. . .so *homely*, she thought—and about as far removed from the minimally sleek lines of her own townhouse as she could imagine.

Callum turned to look down at her, his heart warmed by her instinctive expression of delight. 'Like it?'

'Oh, Callum. . . It's—'

He moved away abruptly, afraid that he was about to do something which not only would be unprofessional in the extreme but something which he would never be able to undo. Like pulling her into his arms and seeking not just comfort there but something much more fundamental. . .

'Sit down and make yourself comfortable,' he told her gruffly, 'and I'll fetch us something to drink. What would you like? Coffee? Or something stronger?'

Nancy drank very little normally and though she would have given the world for a reviving glass of wine right then she didn't dare. Wine would make her feel warm and cosy and relaxed, and all her defences would come tumbling down. And she needed to hang onto her defences right now because they were the only thing stopping her from hurling herself into his arms.

'Coffee, please.'

He nodded and disappeared into the kitchen, where Nancy heard him clattering about as she moved around the sitting room to look at it more closely.

One wall was lined with bookshelves, full to bursting with a collection of volumes which astonished her in their broad range of subjects. There were works of fiction and biographies, science fiction and reference books, poetry and thick volumes of art.

Much of the plain-washed surfaces of the walls were covered with paintings—water-colours for the most part—some depicting local scenes, which she recognised. A couple of the others were by a very well-known artist, not in the prime positions she might have imagined some people would have chosen to draw attention to their obvious cost but hung with care so that the spots chosen reflected the subject matter most advantageously.

She was standing deep in thought, looking at one of them, and didn't hear Callum come back into the room until a slight clunking noise warned her that he had deposited the tray on one of the small, low tables beside the sofa. She whirled round to find him staring at her in a manner she could only describe as slightly dazed.

'Is something wrong?' she asked.

He shook his head. 'Like it?' he asked, coming to stand beside her to look at the painting.

'Who wouldn't?' Nancy responded throatily, thinking that she would honestly pay a month's salary to own a painting as beautiful as that one of the winter sunset but thinking that Steve wouldn't give it house room.

'You'd be surprised,' came his wry rejoinder, remembering how Helen had pronounced his home 'dry' and 'stuffy' and had suggested that he knock through the wall between the sitting room and the dining room, with the solemn advice that this would make his home less 'poky'! 'Sit down, Nancy, and we'll have some coffee.'

The coffee was fragrant, the cups an old-fashioned design in bone china, and there were irresistible, melt-in-the-mouth lemon biscuits which, he informed her, she could buy at the local bakery.

She finished her coffee, then sat back against the cushions on the comfortable, worn sofa and sighed blissfully.

He glanced across the room at her, thinking that fate was indeed cruel. How right she looked, sitting there.

She had removed her navy overcoat to reveal a dress in wool of softest apricot, which brought out the faintest sheen of roses to her cheeks.

He sighed. It was as though his home had been nothing but a house before Nancy Greenwood had entered it. But he quickly pulled his thoughts in line because he had no earthly right at all to question fate, not when that same fate had seen fit to snatch away one of his dearest friends and patients.

And then he remembered exactly what Emma had rather shockingly said just before they left, and wondered whether he should refer to it. But it was too painful to think of Emma so, instead, he remarked, 'So, what inspired the change of car? The new hairstyle? The softer line in clothes, which—I feel duty-bound to tell you—

suit you far more than those austere-looking outfits you used to favour?'

Nancy hesitated. How much should she tell him? She thought of the many weeks that she and Steve had been attending their counselling sessions and of her increasingly curious feeling of detachment. It was as though *she* was going through the motions of trying to act on the conflicts which had been voiced in these sessions but was aware at the same time that, if anything, she and Steve seemed to be drifting further and further apart, instead of pulling together.

And yet she had talked to no one about it, and the urge to confide in someone was overwhelming.

'My marriage was going through a rocky patch,' she admitted, thinking that this sounded far less compromising than saying that her marriage was in desperate trouble. She glanced up at him, her brown eyes wide and candid. 'But you may already have guessed at that.'

Now it was Callum's turn to hesitate. If he had been speaking freely he would have told her that her husband was a waste of space, but it was most definitely not his place to tell her that. For might she not think that his words were motivated by self-interest? Instead, he tried for a non-partisan approach. 'I had picked up several hints that all was not well,' he conceded, with what he hoped was an encouraging and not a prurient smile.

'In the restaurant, you mean?' she asked anxiously, because every one of those present that night had studiously avoided even *mentioning* that disastrous meal.

'And at other times.' He shrugged, recalling telephone conversations she had had with Steve. Conversations that had made him want to take Steve Greenwood by the scruff of the neck and knock some sense into him.

'But most marriages go through bad patches, Nancy—'

'Yes, that's what the counsellor said—' Nancy halted as she realised that she had blurted it out, anyway, then bit her lip in embarrassment. 'We've been going to marriage guidance,' she admitted sheepishly.

So it was serious enough to warrant counselling, he mused. 'Well, as you know, Nancy, I'm a great advocate of seeking outside help. Having an impartial third party present often makes you view things quite differently. Has it helped at all?'

Nancy was torn between loyalty and honesty, and in the end replied with an uncomfortable mixture of both. 'I don't know. . . It's better than it was, anyway.'

'Well, that's good,' he put in heavily.

'Yes.' She found that she was staring at him intently, drinking in every detail of his gorgeous, craggy face. He looked so strong, she thought unwillingly, so dependable. The kind of man who would make a marvellous father.

Her throat constricted with pain. Soon it would be Christmas, and after that her final month.

As if sensing the path of her thoughts, Callum said, 'You still haven't fixed up a job for yourself, have you?'

'No.'

His green gaze was very steady. There had been advertisements in the *BMJ* every week, with some practices close enough for her not to have to move away from the area. 'And you haven't even made any applications or at least, if you have, no one has asked me to provide a reference for you.'

There was no point in denying it. 'No. I haven't.'

'Want to tell me why? You'll be jobless if you aren't careful, Nancy.' He gazed at her questioningly.

She was loath to voice her feelings. That she was unsure of the future of her marriage. Unsure of where she would be living. Unsure whether she had what it took to go into general practice on her own if the marriage *did*, as she suspected it would, fail.

'Oh, I think that my budget can stretch to a few weeks of being unemployed,' she told him brightly. 'And I've got my membership exam to study for, remember? I'm sure that I can grab a locum here and a locum there in order to keep my head above water!'

He nodded. 'You could do holiday relief at our practice, if you like. I know that the others rate you very highly as a doctor—'

'No!' she responded, much too sharply and much too quickly, as she thought of the agony of continuing to work so closely with Callum. Growing fonder and fonder of him day by day and having to watch him settle down with someone totally unsuitable—like Helen Burton—when he should have been settling down with *her*! And then she realised just what it was she had admitted to herself. . .

Callum jerked his head up in surprise, frowning slightly as he looked at her. 'I won't take that personally,' he told her drily, an ironic smile quirking the corners of his mouth, 'though there are more *diplomatic* ways of turning down a job, you know, Nancy!'

Nancy stood up abruptly, knowing that if she didn't get out of there she would compound it all by making a complete and utter fool of herself. 'Callum, I must go,' she told him shakily.

He was on his feet in an instant, his face carefully composed into an expression of concern though his green eyes looked troubled. He moved towards her and took both her hands in his, a gesture which afterwards he tried to convince himself was based solely on friendship.

She let him hold her hands like that, telling herself that it was just the once—that it was perfectly innocent. As a doctor, she had seen him making comforting gestures like this time and time again. But, oh, did his patients experience this sudden, debilitating sensation— as though her insides had turned to jelly and her head to mush? Just the touch of his hand over hers was making her heart sing and her heart thunder. Could something so innocent be so very wrong? She bit her lip in turmoil.

'What is it, Nancy?' he whispered softly, sensing her confusion. 'Is it what Emma said? I can't say that she was delirious because we both know she wasn't. But she is a romantic. She's always been nagging me to get married, and she probably forgot that you're already spoken for. . . Nancy? What on earth is it, Nancy?'

She clamped her lips together and shook her head furiously. Once she had cried in his office, and there had been justification for that. But if she cried now she would end up in his arms, and who knew where that would lead? If she cried now it would be because she loved him, and it was hopeless. He was her trainer and an honourable man, and she was a married woman who believed firmly in commitment.

'I must go, Callum.' She forced herself to say it, even though every word was a lie. 'Steve will be waiting for me.'

CHAPTER TEN

DECEMBER came and brought with it the usual rash of complaints in the run-up to Christmas. It was almost as though the patients decided that if they were ill *before* the yule-tide festival then they wouldn't actually get sick over the rest of the holiday period! Callum and Nancy and the rest of the practice staff were run off their feet, seeing people with colds, flu and chest infections.

'Did you know that a general practitioner's workload *doubles* during the winter months?' Callum asked her one morning.

'I can believe it,' sighed Nancy wearily, having just tried to explain to her fifth patient that a hacking cough did not mean that she was automatically going to prescribe antibiotics.

'It's the cyclical nature of general practice I was telling you about!' Callum joked, though his words had a slightly hollow ring to them as if he was just going through the motions of trying to be amusing. Nancy had to force a smile as she prepared to begin yet another jam-packed surgery.

At least she found the work itself utterly absorbing. She liked the variety as well as the challenge. And, yes, every day she dealt with mundane complaints such as sore throats and ingrowing toenails, and she, like every other doctor, sometimes had her fill of vague presentations and skin infections. But there was also the excitement of being presented with a set of symptoms and a puzzled, unwell patient, and getting to the bottom of the symptoms until she came up with a diagnosis.

And a cure.

'It's just like being a detective!' she exclaimed to Callum one day when she had successfully diagnosed a case of polymyalgia rheumatica.

A man of fifty-five had come into surgery, complaining of pain and stiffness in his shoulders and hips and finding it hard to get going in the mornings. Overall, Nancy had found that his muscles were tender but, for her, the giveaway sign was that he couldn't reach up to the top shelf of his toolshed. An emergency ESR had confirmed her tentative diagnosis and she had prescribed steroids accordingly. The patient had come back two days later absolutely jubilant.

'He called me a miracle-worker!' said Nancy, blushing with pride.

'Did he now?' said Callum teasingly, but his green eyes had been alight with pleasure. 'And a very *busy* miracle-worker, judging by the size of your list.'

'I don't mind,' said Nancy honestly. 'As you said, it's a hectic time of year for the practice.'

But, if she was to be completely honest, she was actually *grateful* to be so rushed off her feet that it gave her little time to think.

Thinking hurt too much.

And the truth was that relations had been more than a little strained between Callum and Nancy ever since that evening at his cottage. It was as though each of them was treading on eggshells. They were certainly being over-sensitive, carefully choosing their words so that no look or gesture which passed between the two of them could be misinterpreted.

Emma had died the day after they had been to visit her, and the surgery had been closed on the morning of the funeral so that all the partners could attend. Nancy had stood shivering in black at Callum's side, the two of them staring in disbelief as the coffin had been lowered into the hard, dark earth and trying to blot out the sounds of muffled sobbing all around them.

At the funeral tea Nancy had gulped down two glasses of sherry in quick succession and had gone looking for Callum. She'd found him crouched on the floor of the downstairs study with Emma's two older children.

They'd all looked up when she'd walked in, and Nancy had been astonished to see Charlotte giggling. She'd been about to beat a hasty retreat, afraid that she might have been disturbing them, but Callum had beckoned to her.

'Come in, Nancy,' he said in his deep voice.

'What are you doing?' she wondered aloud.

'Callum's just showing us the magical snowstorm,' said William in a wooden kind of voice.

'Mummy gave it to him for the surgery,' added Charlotte, 'but he's brought it here for us to keep. Look!'

With the ornament held carefully between two chubby palms, Charlotte passed it over to her, and Nancy took the glass dome and peered into it. She had watched Callum use it to quieten fractious children on many occasions. Inside was a snowman, with brightly striped scarf and a pipe for a nose—it was a very old-fashioned snowman.

She shook it gingerly—for it was very heavy—and flakes of snow began to swirl, almost obscuring the snowman, and then flutter to settle into washing-powder drifts.

The four of them watched in silence.

Callum cleared his throat and spoke with an effort. 'Mummy used to say—'

'That God was crumbling coconut-ice!' piped up Charlotte, sounding uncannily like her mother.

There was a long, oddly comforting silence.

'I don't think I've ever eaten coconut-ice before,' said Nancy hesitantly.

'That's because it's an unfashionable sweet,' smiled Callum. 'A dentist's nightmare.'

William's face was thoughtful. 'But Mummy used to say that it would be a terrible world without coconut-ice, and that if you brushed your teeth properly it would be OK.'

Nancy held her breath as she looked at Callum. It was the first time William had mentioned his mother since she had died.

'And it will be OK,' said Callum softly. 'Honestly, William, it will.'

The small boy looked up at him with hopeful eyes.

'My daddy can make coconut-ice!' squeaked Charlotte.

'Then shall we ask him to make us some very soon?' Callum queried, and they nodded in unison.

He stood and held out two hands, and the children solemnly took one each as they went off in search of their father while Nancy followed behind, still carrying the heavy glass dome.

As the days galloped faster towards Christmas the doctors lost their annual battle to keep decorations down to a tasteful minimum. Soon brightly coloured paper-chains were looped all along the ceilings and garish scarves of glittering tinsel festooned every picture frame. Phillippa muttered a bit when red, white and green balloons and bunches of holly began appearing in all the surgeries, but didn't have the heart to complain about them.

Jenny McDavid's son regularly drove his lorry near one of the county's largest Christmas tree farms, and he appeared one morning just before the health centre opened, bearing an eight-foot-high monstrosity!

'And where are we going to put *that*?' groaned David Davenport, thoroughly exhausted with the night-time demands of two hungry babies and short-tempered as a consequence.

'Where we always put it, of course,' smiled Callum, thinking that it *was* the biggest tree they had ever had! 'In the centre of the waiting room. I'll help Jenny put it up when everyone has gone home, and we'll all lend a hand to decorate it tomorrow. And speaking of going home. . .' he eyed the dark rings beneath his partner's eyes '. . .why don't you knock off now, David? Go home and order a carry-out—'

'A *what*?' piped up Jenny and Nancy in unison behind them.

Callum grinned. 'A take-away, I mean.'

'It's the Scottish in him,' said David kindly. 'It comes out at moments of stress.'

'Aye, it does!' Callum did an exaggerated Scottish accent and made a mental note to ask young Suzy Walters—home on holiday from her nursery-nurse training—to wander up to the Davenports' house to see if they wanted a hand with the babies. It would earn Suzy a few extra pounds, and it might give the Davenports a bit of a break. Because if David was looking tired he wondered how on earth Cassandra would be coping. . .

As the holiday grew closer there was a dip in the number of patients attending surgery as shopping took precedence over health for all but the genuinely sick.

'Shall we go back to combining our surgeries for the moment, then?' asked Callum cautiously one morning. 'As it's fairly quiet.'

'Oh, *could* we?' responded Nancy eagerly, trying to convince herself that every second spent with Callum was a valuable learning experience.

Nothing else.

Mrs Berringer came to see them—a transformed Mrs Berringer, clad most uncharacteristically in jeans and a brightly coloured emerald sweatshirt, on which was smeared something which looked suspiciously like chocolate.

'Charlie and I were making a yule-log together,' she explained, seeing the direction of their bemused gazes. 'I've left him at home with his father—he's been taking more time off work recently,' she concluded, with a beaming smile.

'And how are *you*?' asked Nancy.

Mrs Berringer drew a deep breath. 'I feel like a new person,' she told them candidly. 'I finished my course of tablets and everything seemed to fall into place once I felt better. I stopped worrying about the unimportant things and accepted that noise and mess are inevitable with young children around.

'And once I seemed to relax then Charlie became more relaxed, too, and I found looking after him less of a strain. And then my husband started joining in more, and. . .'

'And?' prompted Callum, with a wide grin. He had

seen that bashful expression often enough to know what was coming next!

'I think I may be pregnant again!' Mrs Berringer blushed. 'Could you give me a test, please, Dr Greenwood?'

A scarcely recognisable Mr Allen came into the surgery to see them, and Nancy could hardly believe that this was the same overweight and unhealthy man with high blood pressure who had come seeking advice on her very first day in practice.

He had brought his wife with him and both were amazingly slim and fit and very, very brown, although their vividly coloured cotton shirts and trousers, emblazoned with palm trees, offered little protection against a freezing winter's day.

'I took your advice, Doctor,' said Mr Allen with a smile as Callum pronounced his blood pressure vastly improved. 'Went on the diet and everything—'

'And I did, too, because I was a real pudding!' confided his wife. 'So we joined the local slimming club, and did quite well—'

'So, well, we won a national competition as Slimmers of the Year!' Mr Allen announced proudly.

'And just got back from a Caribbean cruise!'

'That was the first prize!' added Mr Allen, and slapped a bottle down on Callum's desk. 'So this is for you, Doctor—to thank you. I feel like a new man—'

'And I feel like a new woman,' Mrs Allen put in, with a smile.

'Just make sure you share it with the lady doctor,' said Mr Allen, nodding in Nancy direction as the two of them left the surgery.

'What is it?' asked Nancy, amused as always to be referred to as the lady doctor—she never heard Callum being referred to as the gentleman doctor!

Callum picked up the bottle and screwed up his face as he read out the description. "'Dark, delicious rum with the addition of fresh mango and guava juices and a secret blend of herbs and spices, make this sunny drink an irresistible cocktail".' He threw Nancy a questioning look. 'So what do you think?'

Nancy thought a lot of things but most of them were things she wouldn't dream of telling Callum. Like how much she was going to miss him, and how quickly her last few weeks as his trainee seemed to be speeding by. She tried for a light touch. 'I think it sounds lethal.'

He smiled, his green eyes crinkling deliciously at the corners. 'Want to give it a try?'

'Have you forgotten that I'm driving?' she asked.

'I hadn't forgotten, no,' he answered obliquely. 'You could have a small one or, alternatively, you could have a huge one and let me run you home. To return the favour, if you like.'

Nancy didn't just throw caution to the wind—she hurled it just about as far as it would go. Last time she had refused his offer of a drink and the noble feeling she had experience had lasted precisely two minutes.

So, what the hell? Why *shouldn't* she? Steve would no doubt be out at one of his office Christmas parties. He loved this time of year for precisely the reason that there *were* so many parties going on, and even their counsellor had agreed that he would probably go out much more than was preferable.

Steve had half-heartedly invited her to a couple—on the counsellor's suggestion—but she had refused. She

knew exactly what they were like—everyone seemed
to get disgustingly drunk and spend the evening cracking
jokes to which she was not privy. 'I'd love to try some,'
she said boldly, with a glance at the garishly labelled
bottle.

Callum looked slightly taken aback, as if her acquies-
cence was the last thing he was expecting. But why not?
Their last patients had been in and he was not on call
tonight.

He stood up and fished around in the cupboard until
he found two beakers with little to say in their favour,
other than that they were functional.

He poured Nancy a hefty measure and a minute one
for himself. 'No ice, I'm afraid,' he said, handing her
one beaker. 'Unless you'd like me to go and fetch you
some from the kitchen?'

Nancy rather superstitiously felt that if he left to fetch
ice he would never return so she shook her head. 'No,
it's fine just the way it is.'

There was an uneasy silence while they each took a
sip and then, as if controlled by some giant puppet-
master, each put their beaker down on the table at exactly
the same time and pulled a face.

Callum gazed across the desk at her with raised
eyebrows.

'Too strong.' She wrinkled up her nose, realising that
emotionally she couldn't cope with Callum driving her
home, not when she was feeling this vulnerable.

'Too sweet,' he countered, with a smile. He leaned
back in the chair. 'So, what are you doing for
Christmas, Nancy?'

Trying to hold onto her sanity, she supposed, but she
gave him the bright smile he no doubt expected. 'Steve

and I are going to my parents' house,' she began.

'In Deal?'

'That's right,' she answered, surprised and pleased that he had remembered.

'And will that be fun?'

'Fun?' she queried blankly.

A muscle clenched in his cheek as he observed her reaction. 'Is having fun such a bizarre concept for you, then, Nancy?'

She realised that she risked coming over as some pathetic little victim in his eyes. And there was no way that she wanted *that* to be his lasting memory of her!

She sat up very straight in her chair. 'I imagine that quite a lot of people find Christmas an endurance test instead of fun,' she told him defiantly.

Not at *your* age, he wanted to say, but how could he?

'Unless you happen to be a child,' she finished defensively. 'Why? What are you doing, Callum, which will be so much fun?'

He decided to ignore her spiky tone, just leaned back in his chair and regarded her with a fond eye. 'I'm off to Cornwall,' he told her. 'My elder brother is coming over from America with his four children and my other brother is travelling down from Chorley Wood with *his* brood so I daren't not be there!'

'And what will you do?'

His green eyes glinted. 'It's all very basic and predictable down there. There will be church at midnight on Christmas Eve, of course. And the chores will be divided equally. The men will be forced to chop wood and peel potatoes while the women prepare vast meals to cope with so many hungry mouths!

Then my mother will force us all out for long, long

walks, ostensibly to work off all those vast meals but mainly because she is a great believer in exercise. She says that she and my father have their best conversations over a long hike!'

'It sounds wonderful,' said Nancy, oblivious to the wistful tone in her voice, but Callum heard it loud and clear and found himself wishing that he could just pluck her up and take her with him. He would like to see Nancy Greenwood with her hair windswept, roses in her cheeks from walking and a bit of flesh on those bones from some of his mother's home cooking.

Nothing devious in his desire, of course.

And just who do you think you are *kidding*? mocked a knowing voice in his head.

'It is wonderful,' he said quietly, thinking that it would be truly wonderful if he had a woman like Nancy by his side.

Nancy scrabbled beneath the desk for her handbag. 'I'd better go.'

He frowned, disappointed. He found talking to Nancy like this as satisfying as a hot bath after a long day's work. And they rarely got the opportunity to sit quietly, chatting, undisturbed. 'But you haven't finished your drink,' he observed.

'No. It really *is* quite strong, Callum.'

'But I can drive you home. Honestly.'

He smiled, and his eyes crinkled at the corners in such an irresistible way that she was very close to saying yes—but what was the point? They would have a fantastic hour or so and then she would be left high and dry as she went home to wait for her husband, wondering why she hadn't met a man like Callum Hughes *before* she was married.

And realising that she couldn't blame Steve for rail-roading her into a marriage which time had proved was certainly not a match made in heaven.

No one had been holding a shot-gun to her back. *She* had been guilty of a mentality which said that if you loved a man enough to go to bed with him then those feelings should be strong enough to want to spend the rest of your life with him.

Now she asked herself how she could have been so *naïve*, but at the time her need for so-called 'respect-ability' had been overwhelming. And that was a direct result of her upbringing.

She had always said that if she had children of her own she would bring them up to question their actions, not to follow a course of behaviour simply because it was socially acceptable. As she had done.

But now she simply couldn't imagine having children, and the reason was perfectly simple.

Because the only man whose children she would be proud to bear was unobtainable. And too decent ever to make a pass at another man's wife. . .

She stood abruptly. 'No. Honestly, it's sweet of you to offer, Callum, but I'll drive myself home.'

He stood up too so that he towered over her. Her cheeks were very pale, he noticed, and the soft choc-olate-brown sweater she wore, which matched her eyes, only served to emphasise her fragility. Such delicacy of bone and skin, he thought longingly, and was struck by how *powerful* his urge to protect her was.

But from what? From the man to whom she was legally bound?

Get real, Callum, he thought, she's a *married woman*. 'I'll walk you to your car,' he said, thinking how mech-

anical his voice sounded as he held the surgery door
open for her.

Nancy awoke on Christmas morning to a blinding headache and the sound of fractured snoring.

The headache was a legacy of the largely sleepless
night *she* had endured because of Steve's snoring. He
had single-handedly almost finished a bottle of Scotch
the previous evening, much to the amazement and horror
of her parents who, though they enjoyed a drink as much
as the next person, were moderate with a capital M.

Nancy had caught her mother glancing over at her
with what she could have *sworn* had been a narrow-eyed
look of sympathy. But surely her parents would expect
her to *endure* Steve's behaviour—however intolerable?

They all went through the rituals of Christmas,
although Nancy needed every bit of acting skill she
possessed to appear enthusiastic over the X-rated scraps
of silk and lace underwear which Steve had seen fit to
buy her.

He had given her a huge, suggestive wink and
mouthed 'Later!' across the room at her, and it had been
as much as Nancy could do not to choke with horror.

Apart from her mortification at having to open something so overtly sexual in front of her parents, she was
astounded that he should think she would be pleased to
receive such a present from him—particularly in view
of the way things had been going between the two of
them lately. Because Steve had refused to go to their
last two counselling sessions.

'What's the point?' he had questioned moodily.
'Nothing has changed, has it, Nancy? You still don't
seem to want to go to bed with me—'

'I find it difficult to be in the mood when you're always drunk!' she snapped.

'And you still nag me about my drinking,' he added sourly. 'Which, as I tell you, is quite normal in the industry in which I work.'

Nancy privately doubted it. 'That doesn't make it right, Steve,' she told him, her concern genuine. 'Think of the damage you must be inflicting on your liver! Not to mention your heart.'

And Steve's response to that had been to pour himself another glass and throw her a truculent stare.

Besides, in her parents' house the problems between the two of them only seemed to become magnified. Was it something to do with the fact that they were being observed which made Nancy see how they must appear to others?

Behaviour which she had tolerated from Steve, maybe even allowed herself to condone, now seemed shocking, almost shameful. And she was no saint, either. She was a doctor, as well as a woman, and if she was seriously worried about Steve's alcohol intake then she knew that the answer wasn't to nag or pretend it just wasn't happening. And she had been guilty of both these things.

She had not only been bucking her own responsibility, but she had been guilty of allowing Steve to do the same.

Even so, Nancy forced herself to behave as normally as possible over Christmas. If their marriage was in its death throes then it seemed unfair to inflict that, and all the subsequent fall-out, on her parents, and especially at holiday time.

In fact, her composure slipped only once and that was when she found a small carrier bag with presents from the practice. It was totally unexpected, and Nancy felt unbelievably touched.

They were just little bits and pieces from the receptionists, which they'd bought for all the doctors—chocolates and smellies, and a fridge magnet saying, NANCY'S KITCHEN, as well as various bottles which had been left by the patients.

'How very sweet of them,' said her mother with a smile, immensely pleased for her hard-working daughter. 'They must value you a lot, Nancy.'

Nancy was pink with pleasure. 'Well, I hope so.'

'But they haven't offered you a partnership yet?' queried her father shrewdly.

'Dad, I told you—they have their full complement of partners. They might like me, but that hardly means they're going to create a position for me!'

'So what are you going to do?' persisted her father.

'I don't know,' said Nancy honestly, aware that she had deliberately left her future vague, the reason suddenly dawning on her with shocking clarity.

It was because she didn't know what would happen between her and Steve. Her future now looked extremely cloudy so how could she possibly commit to becoming a partner in *any* practice?

'Look,' said her mother quickly, as if in an attempt to break the rather awkward silence which had descended, 'there's something else in here.'

Nancy dug into the corner of the carrier bag where a tiny package reposed. She willed herself not to react as she saw whose distinctive handwriting was on the label.

'It looks like *jewellery*!' observed her mother quietly.

Nancy looked up quickly to find that Steve's eyes

were trained sharply on her, and she willed her hands not to shake as she opened it.

Inside was a tiny box, containing a pair of small white enamel earrings.

'Oh, they're *snowmen*!' cooed Nancy's mother in delight as she peered at them closely. 'Aren't they sweet? Put them on, Nancy! Who are they from?'

Thinking of Emma, Nancy put them on with trembling fingers. She knew that she would treasure them for the rest of her life. 'They're from my trainer,' she said hesitantly, not seeing the swift, assessing stare that passed from her mother to her father. 'Callum Hughes.'

'They're tacky,' sneered Steve dismissively.

Their eyes met in a long, searching gaze. And it was at that precise moment that Nancy knew her marriage was over.

CHAPTER ELEVEN

JANUARY was the gloomiest month of Nancy's life.

She was aware of time running out—of her days in the practice with Callum being numbered. Also, she was having to cope with the reality of life without Steve.

He had moved out just as soon as they had returned from spending Christmas with her parents, and had demanded that she put the house on the market immediately.

'Let's just sell it,' he had snarled, seeming to grow more like a stranger with every second that passed—leaving her wondering whether there had ever been a bond which had drawn them together in the first place. 'And split the profits as soon as we can!'

Quite frankly, Nancy had needed no second bidding. The house had been Steve's choice and she had absolutely no desire to stay there on her own, even if it hadn't conjured up all kinds of grim memories for her. She, too, wanted the whole sorry affair resolved as soon as possible.

But at work she carried on as though nothing was amiss. January was a busy enough month for people not to notice that she was a little paler than usual and, if they did, no one sought to remark on it.

Her reasons for not wanting to tell Callum were complex, and complicated by her feelings for him—feelings which she knew she ought not to have and which would certainly have horrified him had he been aware of them.

Oh, she wasn't denying that there was an attraction between them. She had made enough mistakes in her relationship with Steve by *pretending* and she wasn't going to do *that* again.

She wasn't a fool and only a fool would have failed to notice that a mutual magnetism existed, but *her* trouble was that she seemed to be muddling it up with love. Imagine how horrified Callum would be to discover that she was labouring under the delusion that she *loved* him—when she had never even been kissed by him! No, it was best to keep quiet about the whole thing.

Callum was counting the days until Nancy left. He had done his best to have a happy Christmas—delighted to be reunited with his elder brother and to meet two new nephews who had been born in New York—but all the time he had been aware of a poignant ache where his heart should have been.

He had spent most nights tossing in mental agony as he imagined all kinds of horrendous scenarios—the worse one being Nancy telling her ghastly husband that she was pregnant and the two of them toasting the future together.

Even his mother had been unable to get to the bottom of it. 'Something's wrong,' she had hazarded in her soft Scottish burr. 'Is it a woman, Callum?'

'Yes,' he said abruptly, with an expression she hadn't seen on his face since he was a little boy of eight and his beloved hamster had died. Mrs Hughes had wisely kept her counsel and interrogated him no further.

Back in the practice he watched his trainee deliver a healthy baby boy and felt an intense kind of rage as she cleaned the baby and swaddled him, before handing him over to a damp-eyed and emotional mother. He found that he simply couldn't rid himself of the disturbing image of Nancy Greenwood, suckling *his* baby at *her* breast.

It was the emotional pain which this recurring thought caused which prompted him to ring up Helen Burton again. He needed to snap out of it! To socialise with other women! God in heaven, he needed to have an *affair*!

He tried to convince himself that the real reason he arranged to meet Helen was to show her that he didn't *always* behave like a boor. He steadfastly refused to heed the small voice which asked him if he was intending to break the habit of a lifetime, by beginning a relationship to which he was not one hundred per cent committed. But Helen Burton was gratifyingly pleased to hear from him and they arranged to meet in a wine bar in Chichester on Friday.

He was late finishing surgery that night and ran into Nancy in the corridor, who coloured pink when she saw him.

'Oh, hi,' he said, wishing that he was meeting *her* in a wine bar.

'Hi!' she responded, wishing that this feeling of intense shyness would disappear. It had been present since Steve had left and seemed to plague her whenever Callum was around, although whether it was caused by the effort of keeping the momentous news of her separation to herself or by a sensation of vulnerability she had no idea.

'Johnny Rink *did* have appendicitis,' she babbled in an effort to fill the awkward silence. 'I admitted him to St Saviour's at lunchtime and they operated on him successfully an hour ago.'

'Good,' he said abruptly, with a not very subtle glance at his watch.

She suddenly noticed a pale green shirt she hadn't seen before and the spanking new emerald silk tie which was knotted around his neck. He looked, she thought wistfully, quite overwhelmingly handsome. 'G-going out?' she queried.

Callum felt fired up with regret and anger. Well, why *not* tell her? She was probably going home to canoodle with that creep of a husband! 'Yes.' He smiled blandly. 'I'm seeing Helen Burton. You remember her?'

'The actress?' Nancy spat the words out.

'That's right,' he agreed, feeling shabby and mean for some inexplicable reason and then getting into a rage again. How *dared* she make him feel bad about having a date with another woman when she was living with Steve?

But when Helen walked into the wine bar two hours later, all blonde and shining beauty—with a figure that made several men choke into their glasses—Callum knew that he would never be able to make love to her in a million years.

And that Nancy Greenwood must be some kind of witch to have cast such a powerful spell on him!

So what started out as an evening during which Callum had intended to woo the lovely Helen ended up with him pouring his heart out to her about Nancy.

Helen Burton was used to male adoration, and Callum's earlier lack of interest had come as a complete surprise to her. Thus, when he had renewed contact she had expected him to be all over her like a rash, and she had allowed herself to idly wonder what it would be like to be married to such a handsome doctor. She was certainly not used to men crying on *her* shoulder!

But, as well as being a competent actress, she was also a very practical woman, and when she realised that Callum was completely smitten by Nancy she tried to think how best to help him. Because, after all, Callum would doubtless have eligible friends!

'And have you *told* her how you feel?' she demanded.

Callum shook his head and gazed sorrowfully into his glass. 'Nope.'

'Well, why the hell *not*? She isn't a mind-reader, is she?'

That third glass of wine was beginning to have some effect. Callum chose his words with all the care of the partially inebriated. 'I can't do that,' he announced.

'Why the hell not?'

'It isn't honourable.'

Helen shook her blonde mane, torn between exasperation and admiration. 'You need to get drunk,' she told him very firmly, thinking of how her three rugby-playing brothers usually sorted out any emotional distress.

So she took Callum home, sat him on the sofa and let him talk and talk about Nancy while she fed him white wine until he fell asleep—long, *long* before any of her brothers would have done, she realised wonderingly.

Then she removed his shoes, covered him with a blanket and left him to sleep soundly all night, there on the sofa.

He woke with a blinding headache, at first not knowing where he was but grateful that Helen had had the foresight to leave an alarm clock set for seven beside him. Had he told her that he had a Saturday morning surgery? he wondered.

Nevertheless, it was a mad dash to get to the practice

on time, and he was grouchy and out of sorts when he arrived.

Nancy, who had had a horrendous sleepless night while she imagined Callum cavorting with Helen, decided to sit in on his surgery, even though it was her weekend off. She didn't care what he thought. She might not ever have him as a man, but she wanted to make the most of the time she had left with him as a doctor. And whenever she was with Callum she learnt something.

She walked into Reception, to find two of the receptionists giggling by the main desk.

'What's the joke?' she asked mildly.

One of the receptionists snorted. 'Just that Dr Hughes came in late for work this morning, which he's *never* done before! And his face was unshaven, and he was *still* wearing the same clothes he had on yesterday! He was in a filthy temper, too!'

'That's enough of that gossip,' reprimanded Jenny McDavid quietly, taking in Nancy's shocked and white face. 'Isn't there something else you could be doing?' She frowned as Nancy turned away. 'Dr Greenwood, aren't you staying?'

'No,' answered Nancy, close to tears but determined not to show it. However, if she didn't get out of there now, at any second she would break down. 'No, I'm not staying.'

Callum, who was nursing the worst hangover of his life and trying to take the temperature of a screaming baby, heard her car roar out of the doctors' car park and correctly guessed the reason for her speedy exit.

And the patients who saw Dr Hughes in surgery that

morning wondered why the normally even-tempered doctor seemed so out of sorts.

For the last few weeks of Nancy's traineeship there existed an uneasy truce between the two of them. Callum found that whenever they needed to talk they approached each other warily, like two prize fighters sizing each other up.

Then one day he drove past Nancy and Steve's town-house and saw the 'For Sale' notice. She had told him that she was leaving the area, yes, but the reality of her departure hit him like a vicious blow to the temple, and he began to long for the day when she would be gone.

For then, surely, he might be able to begin to piece his life together again.

He went to see her after surgery one morning in the week before her departure.

Nancy was scribbling out a prescription for insulin when he appeared at her door. Ignoring the pounding of her heart, she attempted to keep her face neutral.

'Yes, Callum,' she said evenly. 'What can I do for you?'

Quashing the X-rated answer he would have *liked* to have given, he cleared his throat.

'The partners want to know what form you'd like your leaving party to take,' he told her.

Nancy blanched. Ideally, she would have liked to have slipped away quietly—with her tail between her legs—but this, she knew, would be unfair to all the practice staff, who she had grown to like very much during the year she had been there.

'Nothing very fancy,' she said immediately.

'No,' he agreed, sensing her reluctance and wishing

there was some way he could get out of it himself.

'A restaurant, perhaps?' he asked mechanically, trying to act as a responsible trainer would, not a love-sick fool.

'I'd—rather not,' she said, remembering the last time they had all been to a restaurant.

'No,' he concurred, remembering the evening himself. 'Then, perhaps, a few drinks here? In the reception area?'

'That would be fine,' she answered brightly.

'And Steve.' He said the name heavily, with an effort, not caring whether or not she noticed, because Nancy was wasted on a man like Steve and it was about time she realised it. 'Will he be coming?'

The temptation to tell him that Steve had left and was living in Winchester was almost uncontrollable, but Nancy didn't give in to it. It would be a cheap indulgence, designed to have Callum sweep her into his arms, and that would be the wrong thing to do—both morally and practically.

Morally because she couldn't just rely on another man to get her through a sticky emotional patch. And practically because although she was certain that Callum found her an attractive person she was also certain that her feelings for *him* couldn't possibly be reciprocated.

And the last thing she needed right now was a romance which would leave her feeling empty and flat when it ended.

'Er. . .no,' she answered. 'Steve will be working, I'm afraid. And, to be honest, it's never much fun going out to work dos if you're not one of the workers. You always feel a bit of an outsider, don't you?'

'Yes,' said Callum slowly.

Nancy's last day came and the patients were gratifyingly sad to see her go.

'Isn't there any chance you could stay, Dr Greenwood?' asked one old lady who Nancy had been visiting weekly since she had been discharged from hospital.

'Not really, Mrs Ripley,' said Nancy with genuine regret, for she had grown fond of the spirited, ex-head teacher who was virtually crippled with arthritis but refused to give into it. 'There simply isn't a vacancy for me to fill.'

The practice staff all crowded into the reception area once the last patient had gone home. Callum had deliberately elected to be on call so that he would be unable to drink. He feared that even one sip of the mulled wine which David Davenport was dispensing so freely would be enough to loosen his tongue, and have him saying things to his beautiful young trainee which he would live to regret.

The receptionists had provided sandwiches and the nurses and secretaries the sugar-laden gateaux, while the doctors were responsible for the wine and soft drinks.

And whilst Nancy was sad to be leaving, and even sadder to say farewell to the colleagues she had grown to like and respect, she was determined not to be a wet blanket and have that be their lasting memory of her!

So she circulated like a social butterfly, and gaily waded through a plate piled high with calorie-ridden party food. She had a sausage roll halfway to her mouth when she saw Phillippa virtuously nibbling on a piece of carrot.

'Phillippa, you *can't* eat *that*!' she exclaimed. 'Not at my party.'

'But it isn't deprivation,' answered the wiry vegetarian with a grin. 'It's a whole way of life. Honestly, I feel fantastic!'

'Maybe I should try it myself,' Nancy remarked drily, as she watched Callum refilling glasses out of the corner of her eye.

The speeches were kept mercifully short, but her eyes were very bright when Callum handed over an inscribed, solid silver pen and told the assembly very solemnly that Nancy was one of the finest doctors he had ever worked with.

And Nancy was grateful for the patient who bleeped him just at that moment and was sick enough to keep him occupied for the next hour, by which time she'd managed to slip away—aware that by this time tomorrow she would be living in London. The house had been sold, her ties with Tenterdon completely severed.

She need never see Callum Hughes again.

She had racked her brains to come up with an idea of what to buy him as a farewell present, as a way of thanking him for all his hard work, but everything she came up with she had rejected as being unsuitable or completely over the top.

In the end, having scoured the shops in villages for miles around, she found another snowstorm. Not of a snowman this time—she suspected that would be much too poignant—but of a fat and jolly Father Christmas. This she arranged to be delivered to his surgery the following morning, by which time she would be long gone. The note which accompanied it was short and simple.

Callum,

Sometimes the English language seems inadequate, like now, but please know that when I say thank you I mean it from the bottom of my heart.

And Callum read the note and sat looking at the glass dome for a very long time, his eyes blinded by tears.

CHAPTER TWELVE

NANCY began a new life in London, gratified to discover that she could still function like a human being.

She found a small but airy flat in north London and busied herself with locum jobs, while her spare time was spent studying for the membership of the Royal College of General Practitioners.

She tried very hard not to think about Purbrook and the practice, which she missed very much.

Or Callum Hughes, whom she missed even more.

It took every bit of will-power she possessed not to send him something for Valentine's Day, and she very nearly caved in when she saw a fading and beautiful Victorian card in an antique shop which she suspected he would adore as much as she did.

Then she remembered last year—the stack of cards and the lavish bouquet from Helen—and while she couldn't resist buying the card she didn't send it.

She took the examination in May, and two weeks later learned that she had not only passed, but had been awarded a distinction!

'I just can't believe it!' she blurted out to her mother on the phone when she rang her to tell her.

'Well, I can,' said her mother proudly. 'I always knew that you had it in you, Nancy.' There was a pause. 'Is the divorce still going ahead?'

'Of course,' answered Nancy quickly.

'On what grounds?' her mother shot out. 'Or shouldn't I ask?'

'It's natural to want to know,' said Nancy slowly, 'but I just want the quickest divorce possible, with a simple division of assets. I don't want to apportion blame and I don't want any bitterness. What's done is done and it's all in the past now—I just thank the Lord that there were no children. We both need to put it behind us as quickly as possible and get on with the rest of our lives.'

'Yes, you do,' replied her mother, and then, in a casual voice which didn't quite come off, added, 'And what about that rather nice doctor you spoke about—the one who bought you those sweet little snowman earrings?'

Nancy glanced at the mirror above the telephone table for she was wearing them. Not very appropriate for a blazing May evening, true, but she foolishly—*foolishly*—wore them most of the time. 'Callum?' she questioned dully.

'Callum! That's right!' came her mother's ringing tones. 'Do you ever hear from him?'

'Of course I don't hear from him, Mum! He was my trainer—nothing more!' Nancy answered crossly, and much too emphatically. Her mother took the hint and pursued the subject no further.

June dragged interminably, which was an odd experience for Nancy because her birthday was in June and it was usually her favourite month.

She was bored, that was the trouble. She knew that she could no longer keep doing locums and putting off the future. She needed a goal in her life—something to work towards.

The only problem was that she didn't have any idea what that goal might be.

She had just finished cooking supper one balmy Friday evening when there was a ring at the doorbell. She made a small exclamation of annoyance as she surveyed the rapidly cooling stir-fry she had just concocted.

She would ignore it, she decided. It was probably someone selling something, even though she had a notice on the door which told would-be salesmen that she wasn't interested in buying anything. Women on their own were just too vulnerable, she was discovering.

The bell rang again, louder and more peremptorily this time, and Nancy strode towards the door, determined to give whoever it was a piece of her mind.

Until she opened the door and saw that it was Callum Hughes who stood there, and the words died on her lips in conjunction with the soaring beat of her heart.

'Callum!' she exclaimed, unable to keep the joy of seeing him out of her voice.

And Callum, who had been practising keeping his face fixed in a particularly stern, professional sort of expression, just melted when he saw the look of delight on her face. 'Hello, Nancy,' he said slowly, doing his utmost not to appear to be feasting his eyes on her.

Nothing had changed, he reminded himself.

'How did you find me?' she asked him breathlessly.

'I bullied the College into giving me your address!'

Unorthodox, thought Nancy—and immensely flattering. 'Come in!' she urged impulsively.

He looked questioningly over her shoulder, as if expecting Steve to materialise suddenly. 'Am I disturbing you?'

She shook her dark head, her supper forgotten. 'Not at all. Come in!'

He took a deep breath and stepped over the threshold but, although he shut the door behind him, the two of them remained standing rather awkwardly in the narrow hall. 'I should have rung you, I know—'

'So why didn't you?'

He had tried—God only knew how he had tried. He'd picked up the phone innumerable times and had then put it down again, unwilling to settle for just a disembodied voice on the telephone—wanting to see her face and her gentle smile instead. 'I came on impulse.'

'I'm glad you did,' she said instinctively, not caring what he made of *that*, and found that she was unable to stop smiling.

He looked at her now—she was dressed more casually than he had ever seen her before, wearing faded old blue denims and with her tiny feet completely bare. With the jeans she wore a scarlet silk shirt, and the bright colour suited her pale skin and dark hair.

'I read about your exam results,' he told her. 'A distinction, no less!'

Nancy blushed and shook her head. 'I had a very good trainer,' she said modestly.

As her head moved he saw which earrings she was wearing and that, more than anything else she could have said or done, made his heart grow warm. But he had to be prepared to face the worst.

'How's Steve?' he asked, in an odd, rehearsed kind of voice.

Nancy hesitated, but there was no earthly reason to hold back from telling him—not now. 'Steve doesn't live here,' she told him bluntly. 'He never did. He lives in Winchester. And I'm sure it will come as no surprise to you to learn that we're getting a divorce—'

There was no opportunity for further explanation because Callum did what he had been wanting to do since the very first time she had walked into his surgery and into his life.

He took her, unprotesting, into his arms and kissed her very thoroughly indeed. Nancy was so dazed and weakened by the experience that she actually went limp in his arms, and he had to pick her up and carry her into the sitting room—which was a first for him.

And her!

'Stop it!' she giggled, once she had got her breath back and he had sat down very close to her on the sofa. 'Callum, *don't*! You make me feel like some helpless, little—'

'Hmm?' His eyes twinkled. 'Do I?'

'Mmm!' she gurgled back. 'You do!'

'While you, in contrast, make me feel strong and omnipotent. Now, isn't that an interesting and complementary combination?'

Nancy stared deep into his green yes, itching to kiss him again but deciding that she needed a few answers before they went down *that* particular path. 'Callum, why are you here?'

He lovingly fingered a strand of shiny, dark hair. 'Ostensibly to congratulate you on passing your exam and, on behalf of my partners, to ask whether you would consider coming into partnership with us?'

'But there isn't a vacancy!' she exclaimed, even though her heart leapt with joy at the thought of going back to the practice she had loved and missed so much.

'But there will be,' he told her with a smile. 'Phillippa

is expecting her fourth baby, and that has been the push she and Julian needed to head off to the sticks. They're moving to a remote part of Cornwall in the autumn, where Phillippa has found some like-minded people to go into practice with.'

'Gosh!' said Nancy, dazed yet again, and then her eyes narrowed. 'So David wants me to join?'

'Yes, he does. And Phillippa says she wants you as her replacement! And Jenny and Margaret and the rest of the receptionists said that *your* lab forms were the only ones they could read, without getting a hieroglyphic expert in to decipher them, so *they* want you back, too!'

'I see,' said Nancy thoughtfully.

'Then there are the patients,' he continued purposefully, his arguments for persuading her back as fluent as if he'd rehearsed them over and over in the car on the way here. Which, naturally enough, he had. 'You wouldn't *believe* how many people have asked when the dark, pretty doctor is coming back!'

'Oh? Who?' asked Nancy, immensely flattered.

'Well, Mrs Markham, for one. She gave birth to a baby sister for Jack just after you'd left!'

'Let me guess—red curls and a solemn expression?'

'Well, now you come to mention it, yes!' He smiled. 'And Mrs Berringer came in to see me the other day and said she wished it was *you* doing her antenatal care.'

Nancy found herself wishing the same, even as she reminded herself that general practice could be deeply painful as well as deeply rewarding. 'How are William and Charlotte?' she queried softly. 'And the baby?'

Callum hesitated as he thought of Emma's children. 'I can't pretend it's been easy—of course it hasn't because something like that never is. The baby is too young to know what's going on but he misses his mother badly, although less obviously than the older two. But children are resilient, Nancy, and there is so much love and support in the community for them and for John.'

'I can imagine,' said Nancy wistfully, as it hit her just how much she wanted to be back in that strong, close community. So she took all her courage in her hands and turned to the dark-haired man beside her and said, 'There's one person you haven't mentioned in all this and that's *you*, Callum. Do *you* want me to come back and join the practice?'

He decided to be brutally honest with her because this was the most important thing he had ever had to say. 'That depends,' he answered.

'On?'

'On your answer to a question that I hadn't intended to ask you for some time, just in case you thought it seemed inappropriate. But now. . . Oh, Nancy, darling, it seems too inappropriate *not* to ask you because I love you so much. Will you marry me?'

She thought she must have misheard him and gazed at him in confusion.

Oh, Lord! Callum's mouth twisted. Now he had frightened her off! She was only just emerging from an unsatisfactory marriage and here he was, dropping another proposal in her lap! What kind of pushy man was he? He needed to give her time. 'Maybe I should put that differently,' he mused. 'Nancy, darling, would you perhaps consider *living* with me?'

Nancy shook her head. 'No, I wouldn't,' she said firmly.

'You wouldn't?'

'No.'

He had done it again! He mustn't rush her. One slow and steady step at a time. It sounded rather old-fashioned and ridiculous to say it, but say it he must. He cleared his throat. 'Will you...um...have a relationship with me, then?' No, that didn't sound right, either. 'Be my girlfriend?' he ventured.

Nancy could have kissed him. In fact, she leaned forward and she *did* kiss him, which made him look all the more confused when she shook her head firmly and said, 'No!'

'*No?*'

'No. I liked your first suggestion best. *I* want to marry *you* because I love you, too—I always have!' She bit her lip and rushed on to try and convince him that she wasn't being flighty. 'Oh, I know what you're probably thinking, Callum—that I've been married once before and I got it wrong so what's going to be so different about this time—?'

He halted her with a finger to her lips. 'Nancy, shh! You don't have to explain or to justify anything to me, my darling. I just know how I feel about you—it's as natural as breathing. Here.' And he solemnly placed her hand over his heart, where she could feel it thundering beneath her palm.

'I love you, Nancy Greenwood. I think I've always loved you. When I met you for the first time I had the distinct feeling that we were meant to be together—call it fanciful, if you like, but it's true.'

He cupped her chin in his hand so that she was caught in the emerald fire of his gaze. 'You made a mistake in your marriage, yes, but you didn't just turn your back on it when so many would have done. You *tried* to sort it out, and when that didn't work you ended it before you dragged one another down too much. That's OK. We've all had relationships that haven't worked out. It's just that most of them don't end in marriage.'

His words jogged a bitter memory. 'You mean, like you and Helen?'

He shook his head. 'The sum total of my relationship with Helen after that disastrous restaurant meal was a night when I talked about nothing but you, got rather drunk and passed out on her sofa. She couldn't understand why I wouldn't tell you how I felt about you.'

'And why didn't you?'

He smiled. 'Honour, I guess. An old-fashioned word, I'm afraid.'

'But a *wonderful* one!' She grinned happily.

He pushed an errant lock of hair away from her mouth and resisted the desire to kiss it again while he asked his next—reluctant—question. 'And how *is* Steve, by the way? Do you have much contact with him?'

'Only through solicitors. I've heard on the grapevine that he's seeing someone else, but I've cut all ties with him and that's the way *he* wants it, too. I haven't seen him since just after Christmas.'

Callum frowned. 'In January, you mean?'

Nancy shook her head. 'No, darling,' she whispered gently. 'Earlier than that. Steve left Tenterdon while I was still working at the practice.'

He stared at her. 'Then why on earth didn't you *tell* me?'

'Because my situation was unresolved,' Nancy told him honestly. 'I felt that I needed time to sort my life out. And because. . .' Her voice tailed away, embarrassed.

'Because?' he prompted.

Oh, what the hell! thought Nancy. 'Because I didn't

just want to have a quick fling with you, Callum. With you it had to be more—much more than that!'

'So does that mean you're going to come back to Purbrook and be my partner—professionally as well as personally?' he asked.

'Yes, I am,' she told him softly. 'And I want you to know that I'm going to be the best doctor you've ever had!'

His amused glance spoke volumes. 'Oh, really?'

'Callum!' Nancy blushed. 'I *meant* that I promise to really care for all our patients.'

'I know you did, my darling,' he told her proudly, before fixing her with a gaze which was luminous with love. 'While I promise to give *you* all the care in the world.'

She closed her eyes and sighed with pleasure, stretching her arms above her head like a cat that has found a perfect place in the sunlight, and when she opened them again she found that he was watching every move she made.

His gaze raked lovingly over her as the action caused the soft folds of the silk shirt to outline the firm swell of her breasts. 'Did I ever tell you that I like you best in these kind of clothes?' he queried huskily.

'You didn't. But that's rather convenient, darling, because so do I! The designer suits were like the car, courtesy of my husband—but no more. End of subject,' she told him softly, putting her marriage firmly into the past where it belonged.

His eyes glinted as he removed first one and then the other snowman earring and laid them carefully on the inlaid coffee-table next to the sofa before he turned to face her, his eyes suddenly serious as he posed a strictly hypothetical question. 'And if I hadn't come looking for you?'

Nancy smiled as his hand began to caress the silky skin beneath her shirt. Then—one day—she would have gone looking for *him*.

And she would tell him that.

One day.

4 FREE
books and a surprise gift!

We would like to take this opportunity to thank you for reading this Mills & Boon® book by offering you the chance to take FOUR more specially selected titles from the Medical Romance™ series absolutely FREE! We're also making this offer to introduce you to the benefits of the Reader Service™—

- ★ FREE home delivery
- ★ FREE gifts and competitions
- ★ FREE monthly newsletter
- ★ Books available before they're in the shops
- ★ Exclusive Reader Service discounts

Accepting these FREE books and gift places you under no obligation to buy, you may cancel at any time, even after receiving your free shipment. Simply complete your details below and return the entire page to the address below. *You don't even need a stamp!*

YES! Please send me 4 free Medical Romance books and a surprise gift. I understand that unless you hear from me, I will receive 4 superb new titles every month for just £2.30 each, postage and packing free. I am under no obligation to purchase any books and may cancel my subscription at any time. The free books and gift will be mine to keep in any case.

M8XE

Ms/Mrs/Miss/Mr...................................Initials ....
                                                                    BLOCK CAPITALS PLEASE

Surname ....

Address ....

....

....Postcode...............................

Send this whole page to:
THE READER SERVICE, FREEPOST, CROYDON, CR9 3WZ
(Eire readers please send coupon to: P.O. BOX 4546, DUBLIN 24.)

MILLS & BOON®

Medical Romance™

COMING NEXT MONTH

SOMEONE ELSE'S BABY by Jean Evans

All Neil was asking of her was friendship but Beth knew that accepting would be a lie. After all her feelings had little to do with friendship.

DANIEL'S DILEMMA by Maggie Kingsley

Daniel had already tried marriage once and he thought it would take a miracle to get him to try it again. And then he met Rebecca...

FROM THIS DAY FORWARD
by Laura MacDonald

Book 2 in the Matchmaker Quartet

Kate had a successful professional life but she fell apart when it came to men! She doubted that Jon would be the one to alter that, but he had other ideas.

A LITTLE BIT OF MAGIC by Josie Metcalfe

When Penny turns up, Dare thinks that she is following him. Little does he realise that she is his new nurse. After such a bad start Penny was determined that things could only get better.

On Sale from **6th April 1998**

Available at most branches of WH Smith, John Menzies, Martins, Tesco, Volume One and Safeway